THE HORSEMEN

FOUR MODERN TALES OF THE APOCALYPSE

THE HORSEMEN

FOUR MODERN TALES OF THE APOCALYPSE

EDITED BY
R.E. SARGENT
STEVEN PAJAK

THE HORSEMEN
(Four Modern Tales of the Apocalypse)
Edited by R.E. Sargent & Steven Pajak

Published by Sinister Smile Press, LLC,
a Division of Crystal Lake Publishing

P.O. Box 637
Newberg, OR 97132

www.sinistersmilepress.com
www.crystallakepub.com

Trade Paperback ISBN: 978-1-964398-80-8

CONTENTS

MARK OF THE BEAST   1
Nikki Noir

W.A.R. GAMES   85
Steven Pajak

LIMOS   163
Megan Stockton

FADE TO BLACK   219
R.E. Sargent

ABOUT THE AUTHORS   299

Conquest (White Horse)

Then I saw when the Lamb broke one of the seven seals, and I heard one of the four living creatures saying as with a voice of thunder, "Come!" I looked, and behold, a white horse, and he who sat on it had a bow; and a crown was given to him, and he went out conquering and to conquer.

—Revelation 6:1–2

MARK OF THE BEAST

NIKKI NOIR

D r. Hale secured an electrode on Tyler's forehead. "Okay, Mr. James. Everything is in place. How do you feel?"

Tyler gripped the arms of the chair as his knuckles went white. "Good."

"There's no need to worry," the lab tech said. "The electrodes will monitor your brain activity in real time while we test the efficacy of your AI implant. We'll ask you a series of questions, and then you'll be on your way."

"Hey, I'm getting free tech for this test." Tyler chuckled. "Can't be that bad."

Dr. Hale smiled. He knelt next to Tyler, pulling the wrist restraints tight. "That's the spirit."

With Tyler secured in his chair, Dr. Hale returned to the control room and activated the intercom. "Remember, I can hear you as well as you can hear me. If you feel anything out of the ordinary, tell us immediately."

Tyler let out a nervous chuckle as he clenched and released his hands. "Do the restraints need to be this tight?"

"Here we go in three, two…" Dr. Hale mouthed "one" silently as he pointed to his assistant, Sabrina. Her finger was positioned above a glowing red button, and as soon as she saw the doctor's motion, she plunged her finger down on the button.

"Still doing good, Mr. James?" Dr. Hale asked.

"You betcha, doc."

The testing team watched through the observation window with bated breath as the device in his arm was activated. Despite the doctor's assurances, they had no idea how Tyler was going to react to the technology. Timelines were tight, technicians were scarce, and non-human subjects had been their primary mode of experimentation until now.

Dr. Hale switched off the intercom and addressed his

team. "So far, so good. It's time to administer the test questions. Prepare the code, Vic."

"On it." Victor's fingers flew across the keyboard.

"Some of these questions are so bizarre," Sabrina noted. "What's the point?"

"There are baseline questions," Dr. Hale replied. "Then legitimate test questions, with random nonsense to help keep the user engaged. In the end, we want to make sure the reported sensations align with—"

"Done, Dr. Hale." Victor slammed the enter key for added gravitas.

The team turned their attention back to Tyler. This moment, as rushed as it was, had been years in the making. Failure was not an option. The product would launch soon, and when it did, the world would never be the same. Sure, it was on the heels of some rubber stamping and timeline fraud, but all great leaps in human innovation are.

Tyler opened his mouth to address the team, but his jaw hung open.

"Mr. James," Dr. Hale kept his voice calm over the intercom, "what are you feeling right now?"

Tyler's eyes fluttered, and his head dropped to the side. Involuntary spasms pulled at his muscles, caused his body to convulse into erratic and unnatural positions. The monitor behind him beeped as his vitals plummeted, red numbers flashing on its screen.

"Sir, his heart rate is dropping," the lab assistant said.

"No, no, no…" Dr. Hale rushed out of the observation room to Tyler's side. "This can't be happening." He tapped Tyler's face. "Mr. James, can you hear me? Please, God, tell me you hear me."

Tyler's eyes shot open; his back straightened. "Yes, Dr. Hale, I can hear you." He lifted his head to face the doctor.

"All part of the process," Dr. Hale said, swallowing his panic.

The doctor made note of Tyler's initial reaction. It was clear some tweaking would be needed. Perhaps a gradual startup as the nervous system interfacing caused shock to the system. But as the doctor and his team continued to monitor Tyler, they noted his symptoms quickly improving. The monitor beeped at greater intervals as Tyler's vitals returned to normal.

"Do you feel any different?" Dr. Hale asked.

"Yes," Tyler answered in a bold voice. "Clearer… Stronger."

"That's perfect. Are you comfortable?"

"I would be a lot more comfortable if you removed these restraints."

Dr. Hale turned to his team. "Please confirm all brain activity and vitals have normalized." He turned back to Tyler and tapped on his notebook. "I don't want to loosen your restraints just yet, in case you experience a fit while your body adjusts to the new currents. We'll perform the interview, and by the time we're done, we should be in a good place to release you."

The interview questions were varied and tedious, taking up the better part of a half hour. During the questioning, Tyler's vitals remained in check. His answers and emotional responses, both external and internally monitored, in unison.

"Last question," Dr. Hale said, satisfied with the results. "What do you become in the end?"

"More than I was yesterday," Tyler replied, his voice detached but firm.

"Perfect." Dr. Hale scribbled a checkmark and called for his assistant. "Let's get Mr. James disconnected from the monitors and out of these straps."

Tyler remained still while the lab assistant pulled the sticky electrodes from his forehead. One pulled off a flap of skin, leaving a red welt.

"Sorry. Are you okay?" she asked. "These can really latch on to you."

"I'm fine."

"Good." She loosened the wrist restraints and stepped aside, offering her hand to help him.

Tyler jumped from his seat with a surge of energy. He knocked the assistant on her ass and ran past Dr. Hale, throwing open drawers and cabinets until he found what he was looking for. A scalpel.

"Make it stop," Tyler pleaded. "I have to make it stop."

"Grab him!" Dr. Hale yelled.

Sabrina, Victor, and Dr. Hale swarmed Tyler, wrestling to gain control of the scalpel before he could hurt himself. In a show of inhuman strength, Tyler swung his arm, sending all three of them flying across the test chamber.

Dr. Hale picked himself off the floor, his hands raised in surrender. "Mr. James, put down the scalpel. Let's talk about this."

"I need it to stop!" Tyler cried, unable to pacify himself. "I don't want this. I never wanted it."

"We can help you."

Tyler shook his head, pausing for only a second before he launched the scalpel into his eye. His cornea released a sickening squelch, accompanied by a deluge of fluid, which poured down his face as the punctured eyeball deflated like a popped balloon. His knees buckled as he faded from consciousness. Then he crumpled to the ground, falling face first onto the floor. The impact of the hard tile drove the scalpel clear through his brain. Tyler convulsed one last time, like a dying animal.

"WE GOTTA GO, DAD. HURRY UP," AVERY GRAVES shouted down the hallway while she rushed around the kitchen, trying to organize her work papers into the appropriate folders. Nothing was more important to Avery than this job, nothing except her dad.

Working for QuestX was a dream, one she had been chasing for years now. With their latest and greatest invention, the Intelli Artificial Intelligence device, on the verge of release, they needed someone to promote them on a global scale. Avery's education and training made her the perfect candidate when the position of Media Relations Director was posted just three months ago.

The money was life changing, but she didn't need it for herself. Growing up poor, she had learned young to live within her means. Her mom, her hero, had dedicated her life to helping others, and after she passed, Avery tried every day to follow in her footsteps. Whether that meant volunteering at food kitchens, organizing fundraisers, fostering animals, or planting trees in the city, she tried to do at least one thing per day to give back.

Whenever she could, she dragged her dad along too. Stephen Graves was a man of few words and disabled, though he had a huge heart. As big as it was dysfunctional. His heart condition meant frequent doctor visits and expenses for Avery. That was why QuestX's salary and flexible work schedule were so important to her. They allowed her to keep his health on track. One day, she hoped to be able to afford one of the IntelliCoreAI devices for him. That way she wouldn't have to wonder about his health. The implant would allow them to be proactive rather than reactive with his medical conditions.

"Dad! We're going to be late." Avery stuffed the folders into her bag. She gathered the dirty dishes from the table. Her phone buzzed, and she pulled it from her pocket, seeing the battery percentage to zero percent right before the screen went black. Dead. *Wonderful,* she thought, frustrated that she had forgotten to charge her phone last night.

"Come on, Dad."

"I'm comin', I'm comin'." Stephen rolled his wheelchair into the kitchen, stopping in the entryway to rub his knees. "Damn rain always makes 'em worse." He glanced up at Avery with a tired smile.

She leaned in and kissed his forehead. "I'm sorry. I don't mean to rush you. You know, the IntelliCoreAI device could help predict the weather and administer electrical stimulation in advance so you don't wake up with sore knees."

"Yeah, yeah, you know how I feel about them tech things." He waved her off. "I know you're just excited to get to your fancy new job, so proud of you."

"I've got the morning off," she said. "I'm worried about you not getting to your appointment."

Avery wheeled her father out to the car and got him situated in the passenger seat for the long drive to his pulmonologist's office. The appointment was uneventful, at least, a standard checkup for his chronic obstructive pulmonary disease. Afterward, Avery dropped him and the car back off at home before she headed to work.

Living in New York City, it didn't make sense to drive the four blocks to the office, especially when the weather was so beautiful at this time of year. With time left before she was scheduled to arrive at the office, she stopped at her new favorite coffee shop for a drink.

"Medium hot caramel latte and a black coffee with two sugars, please."

Avery quite enjoyed walking to her office. The familiar noises of the city, a bother to some, were comforting to her. Every day, she followed the same path to work, and every day, she looked for the sweet homeless man Frank near the encampment.

She had met Frank three months prior when she began working at QuestX, and since, she never passed by him without stopping. He never asked her for anything, but whenever she could, she brought him coffee, food, or gave him whatever cash was in her pocket. It wasn't much, but it was the one part of her morning that felt like it mattered more than the rest. At least it was an action that had a direct and immediate impact.

Frank stood on the edge of the curb holding a cardboard sign as she approached.

Behold, the rider on the white horse has come
With a crown upon their head and a bow in their care
The seals are broken, the conqueror is unleashed

And all shall fall beneath their reign, for the end is near

"Wow, Frank. Deep." Avery handed Frank his black coffee and smiled at his peculiar sign.

"The end of times," Frank insisted. "It's coming. You need to prepare."

"I'd love to, Frank, but I'm about to be late for work. I'll see you later."

As she walked through Times Square, her boss, Sloane King, appeared high above her head on a massive digital billboard. Sloane was dressed in her signature stark-white blazer set and the gold Tiffany bow necklace she wore every day. "This is the future," Sloane announced. "The future you want for your children, for your children's children. Tomorrow will hold a world that is better than the one you live in today. Because *you* will be more than you were yesterday."

Avery smiled. As QuestX's media director, it would never get old hearing her boss, one of the wealthiest women in the world, recite the words she had prepared. It was as if every commercial, billboard, and advertisement had Avery's signature plastered on it, and it made her feel alive. She turned away from the billboard and hurried to work, ready to begin another day of promotional work.

THE ELEVATOR DOORS TO THE 62ND FLOOR PARTED, opening to the hustle and bustle of QuestX. For some reason, the hustle was more frantic than usual. People walked briskly by, keeping their heads down, while others exchanged hushed whispers. Avery didn't get more than five steps off the elevator when her boss' assistant rushed to her side.

"Avery, where the hell have you been?"

"With my dad. I cleared it with Sloane. He had an appointment."

"This company is your priority."

"I know that, I—"

"Didn't feel like answering your phone," the assistant said and, without pause, continued. "Give me your coffee. No drinks in the conference room. Anything else you need me to take to your office? Pile it on. There's no time to waste. Everyone is waiting for you."

"Me… What's going on?"

"I can't say." The assistant's voice was strained.

Avery handed over her coffee cup, then shrugged off her coat and slung it over the assistant's arm, pulled out her laptop, and tucked it under her arm. Everyone in the conference room stared in silence as she threw the door open and stumbled inside.

"Thanks for joining us," Sloane said as Avery regained her composure.

"Sorry, my phone died and—"

"Quiet." Sloane directed Avery's attention to the TV.

"This is Dr. Hale and his team at our testing facility. Now, Dr. Hale, please give Avery a recap of what happened today, since she has finally decided to join us."

Dr. Hale hung his head. "We had a situation at the testing facility this morning. There were some unforeseen side effects of the activation on our test subject, Tyler James. I regret to inform you that the test subject is deceased."

"Deceased," Avery repeated. "We've tested this before, right?"

"We've performed tests." He paused. "This was unexpected…violent."

The female lab assistant standing behind Dr. Hale whimpered, then wiped a tear from her face. Despite the poor quality of the video call, the horrified expressions on their faces were clear.

"We'll need a full report. Spare no details. We need to get this contained as soon as possible. I need a list of individuals affected, everyone with knowledge of the test, family, and friends of the deceased." Sloane directed her attention to a woman standing next to Avery in the conference room. Avery recognized her as a member of the legal team. "Get NDAs out to all the individuals who witnessed or have knowledge of this event."

"Yes, ma'am," the legal rep replied.

"Dr. Hale," Sloane hardly paused for a breath, "brief Avery on the specifics, so she can find the best way to present this to the media. Avery, you need to draft a press release and get it to me within the hour." With that, Sloane left the room, letting the glass door slam behind her.

Avery stared at the monitor for a moment. "Okay, Dr. Hale, give me the details."

Dr. Hale opened his notebook and scanned the page. "We began testing the IntelliCoreAI implantable device at four a.m. this morning. The test subject, Tyler James, received his implant the night before and had just risen from an eight-hour sleep cycle. His sleep was monitored in our lab, and no anomalies were detected. Our goal was to monitor the first successful human implant activation in real time to ensure nothing unexpected occurred…"

"Did his body reject the implant?" Avery asked.

"There was a concern: his body's ability to adapt to the speed and intensity of the integration. We will need to slow the integration process before a mass release. But that issue resolved itself."

Avery folded her arms over her chest. "Then why is the test subject deceased?"

"He killed himself," the lab assistant, Sabrina, blurted out.

Dr. Hale put his hand on the lab assistant's shoulder. "The test subject was not forthcoming with his mental state. He was suicidal."

Sabrina choked. "When the device integrated with his mind, it brought his desire for self-harm to the forefront and motivated him to accomplish it."

"This should not have happened. All of our code configurations were reviewed, tested, and approved. We can fix a compromised app. What we can't do is be held accountable for someone's unreported mental illness. That's your story."

"This doesn't look good," Avery said, scribbling the explanation down in her notebook.

Before Dr. Hale could continue, a commotion broke out in the lab. Avery couldn't hear any details over the shouting, but she watched on the lagging display as everyone scrambled. Men dressed in black combat gear marched into the camera's view a moment later, and soon after, the video call was disconnected.

"The Rhode Island facility was just infiltrated." Avery rushed into Sloane's office, trying to catch her breath. "Dr. Hale—"

Sloane waved her hand in the air, motioning Avery to sit down and shut up. Her ear was plastered to her cell phone. "Okay… Yes… That's what I said." Sloane spoke into the phone receiver with a commanding tone.

Avery couldn't make out the voice on the other end, but it quieted in resignation as Sloane ended the call.

"I'm aware the facility was hit," Sloane said, leaning

back in her chair. "I didn't realize it would happen so fast." She looked impressed. "I'll have to give the enforcers a raise."

"The enforcers?" Avery asked. "Did we break into our own facility?"

"When tragedy strikes, it's every man for himself." Sloane paused. "We needed to ensure the evidence was secured." She looked at her watch. "I asked for that press release in an hour. Did you get what you needed from Dr. Hale before the raid?"

Avery nodded.

"Good, that leaves you with just over a half hour left. Better get back to it."

Twenty minutes later, the press release was ready. When you work for a company as big as QuestX, with a leader as connected as Sloane King, things have a way of getting done. Sloane was well connected; her father Marshall King was the wealthiest tech mogul the world had ever known, and she wasn't far behind.

Avery used her position as Sloane's media director to request information that would not be made available to most people, namely Tyler James' medical records. She couldn't release them, but she wanted to do her due diligence in determining the root cause and planning how to address the public.

Sloane had doubled down on Dr. Hale's position. "Just focus on Tyler's undisclosed mental illness," she said before Avery left her office. Avery did as she was told and got a release draft emailed to her boss in the timeframe requested, but the situation didn't sit well with her.

As she pondered this question, an email came in with the classified health information of Tyler James. She combed through the very average-looking files, finding none from any mental health professionals or facilities. Additionally, his primary care information referenced nothing about mental health.

Her stomach turned as she considered getting up on stage, in front of the world, and holding a press release based on something that may not be true. But a company like QuestX didn't have the luxury of ignoring a death. The world would soon know about Tyler James, and they would demand answers.

Avery called her boss on Zoom. "I've been looking into Dr. Hale's story, and I'm seeing gaps."

"Are you the legal team now?" Sloane asked.

"No, I just—"

"Drove outside of your lane. Your job was to listen to the doctor and send me a press release. Your job ended when you did that. Whatever this is, this digging, it's the furthest thing from what you should be doing. I need you up on that stage, looking like a goddamn angel, and explaining why this was not our fault."

The call disconnected, and Avery found herself stunned. This was not the behavior she was used to, but these were the trying times that pushed people to their limits. These were also the times when a Media Director had to step up and help the company survive. In the interest of the product.

Avery fixed her blazer in the mirror and applied another coat of lipstick. As the face of QuestX, she had to look perfect. She had to convince the world that this was nothing, a blip. That the company would forever ensure additional testing is performed, and that only well-vetted, willing subjects will ever be used for testing of the Intelli Artificial Intelligence devices. She straightened and took a deep breath, hoping she could convince herself of those things while she was convincing the crowd.

"Good morning, and thank you for joining us today." Avery paused as she looked out at the large crowd of reporters, journalists, and cameramen. It was even more crowded than she expected, but she swallowed the lump in her throat and continued. "We are here to address the incident that occurred at QuestX's Rhode Island testing facility. First and foremost, QuestX, the King family, and I want to express our deepest condolences to Tyler James' family. We understand the impact this tragedy has had and take full responsibility for not validating the survey filled out by Mr. James prior to the incident."

She stepped out from behind the podium, a knot in her stomach as she prepared to lie to the world. The faces before her were transfixed, what felt like a million eyes staring at her. The weight of their unanswered questions hanging on her heart.

"Our number one priority is to be transparent with the world. Our customers, stockholders, and friends deserve that much. We will talk in depth about the facts, outline the steps we've already taken to address this issue, and how we will take measures to prevent anything like this from occurring again." She pressed a button on the remote, changing to a live feed on the jumbotron mounted behind her.

"You might be wondering why Sloane King herself isn't present today." Avery pointed at the jumbotron, which showed a drone shot of Sloane King pulling up to a house in her white Mustang. Sloane walked to the front door, a white envelope in her hand. She knocked on the door, and a woman answered. Then a disgruntled man walked up behind the woman. He appeared to be shouting. Avery flicked the TV back to the QuestX logo.

"Sloane just delivered a one million dollar check to the Tyler James family. His wife, Charity, and his brother Tommy will not have to worry about any funeral costs, or any costs whatsoever, for the foreseeable future. This million-dollar check is in addition to Tyler James' considerable compensation for testing with us."

Journalists and reporters hopped to their feet, waving their arms and shouting questions at Avery. "Why would they want an implant after what happened?" one asked.

"Tell us what happened to Tyler," another added.

"Hold your questions until the end, please. If anything is left unanswered, you may ask me at the end of the presentation."

Avery took a deep breath and closed her eyes. When they opened, so did her mouth, speaking words she wished would stay inside. She brought Tyler's alleged mental history to light at Sloane's direction. She explained that when the product interfaced with Tyler's mind, due to his undisclosed condition, there was an inherent risk. QuestX was therefore unable to account for this risk or build safeguards around it.

"This product is still in testing," Avery continued. "The safeguards I'm referring to exist, but they weren't in place yet because they were considered unnecessary for this subject. Trust me when I tell you that QuestX puts the safety of their customers first. There are additional screening measures being put in place, such as surveys that ask questions in multiple ways to discern inconsistency in answers and determine if we are dealing with someone who may have a mental illness. That is, of course, moot, as the self-harm safeguards are being integrated with the product as we speak and will alert us to subjects who have suicidal thoughts."

The reporters were jumping through their skin, but one question was projected above the rest. "The product caused Tyler to kill himself?"

"Remember, IntelliCoreAI interfaces with your neural connections. It translates your needs, wants, and desires. Then it adjusts the chemical balance and frequencies in your brain for enhanced motivation to achieve them. The device can, and will, detect suicidal thoughts and behavior and, through its interface, actively prevent self-harm. This product is, by design, meant to prevent death and harm to the wearer. Specifically, it scans and reads your body, predicting disease, illness, and future medical problems years, sometimes decades, before diagnosis. I could go on and on, but I'll save that for our product launch next month."

Avery exhaled, watching the faces before her transform as they accepted her answers. Sure, the reporters were still shouting questions, but the audience was sated, and Avery was thankful to be done with the worst part of her job. She was still proud to be associated with this product that could do so much good for the world, that could save so many lives. But given the unanswered questions surrounding Tyler's death, a seed of doubt had been planted in her mind. How far was Sloane willing to go to get this product to launch?

A MONTH LATER, AVERY WAS BACKSTAGE AT THE GALA with Sloane and her father, tech mogul Marshall King. The event was like nothing she had ever witnessed before. She scanned the crowd through gaps in the flowing velvet curtain while Sloane presented.

The ballroom was packed with only the most elite—celebrities, investors, and influencers, all buzzing with excitement about the big reveal.

Long before Avery joined QuestX, she had followed the IntelliCoreAI journey from ambitious tech concept of the future to a device that would present in her lifetime, a true miracle of dedication. It was a life-altering technology with boundless applications designed to boost cognitive abilities, monitor and aid patients with various health ailments, and provide real-time information on the environment, directions, anything and everything you could imagine. But at $500,000 per device, the IntelliCoreAI was only accessible to the wealthy.

Avery hung on every word of Sloane's presentation; Sloane delivered her words with expert precision. She knew exactly what to say to these people and exactly how to say it.

"Exclusive," Sloane shouted from center stage. "You

are the only people who will be able to flaunt the latest and greatest technology."

Until the secondary model comes out, Avery thought.

QuestX had a lower price point model in mind, once everyone who could afford IntelliCoreAI paid full price, of course. The idea with the secondary model was to make up the money and then some over the course of a lifetime with transactional charges. Need the technology to do something this instant? Okay, but it's going to cost you ten bucks. You don't have the money; the device doesn't do what you want. This is in contrast to the presented model, a one-time purchase with unlimited use.

Sloane tossed in buzzwords and business phrases whenever she could, tugging on the ears of the prolific. Things like future proof, customizable, prestigious, transformative. The audience whispered excitedly every time she finished a sentence.

"IntelliCoreAI is a beast," Sloane concluded. "An unstoppable force of innovation in a world that has no idea what's about to hit it." She picked up a champagne flute. "The future waits for no one. IntelliCoreAI is available to those bold enough to claim it. Don't be left behind." Sloane raised her glass to the crowd as they burst into applause. "Welcome to the next phase of human evolution."

Sloane pivoted and walked backstage, joining Avery and Marshall.

"Delivered perfectly," Avery said with a smile.

"She did well," Marshall admitted. "But there is plenty of room for growth."

"Ignore my father." Sloane tossed back her champagne and handed Avery the empty glass. Then she checked her phone. "We already have one thousand three hundred twelve preorders, Dad, and that's not including the one you just had implanted."

"Well, you're my daughter," Marshall scoffed. "I felt like I had to."

"Just you wait," Sloane said. "Soon the only King these people will recognize is me."

"You killed it," Avery said.

"Yes, I did." Sloane smiled at Avery. "For our meeting tomorrow, bring the media outreach strategy and press kit. We need—"

"Sorry, one moment." Avery pulled her phone from her pocket. She had missed several calls during the presentation, and her phone was ringing again. She didn't recognize the number, but the persistence concerned her. "These people won't leave me alone… Hello?"

"Is this Avery Graves?"

"Yes, who is this?"

"I'm a registered nurse at Manhattan Memorial Hospital. Your father, Stephen Graves, has been admitted. You're listed as his emergency contact; we need you to come in right away."

AVERY RUSHED STRAIGHT TO THE HOSPITAL, WHICH was not as quick as she hoped, given the evening traffic. She got his room number from the front desk and ran to his room.

"Hey, Angel," Stephen Graves said weakly.

"Daddy." Avery rushed to the side of the hospital bed. "Are you okay? They didn't tell me anything over the phone. What happened?"

"Calm down, I'm fine."

"You're in the hospital, Dad, you're not fine."

"I was just eatin' lunch on the couch, watchin' my show. Couldn't catch my breath. I thought I might pass out, so I called. Ambulance came to pick me up, told me I was having a heart attack, tried telling me I need all kinds of help."

"A heart attack? Jesus, Dad." She placed her hand on his arm and sat next to him.

"You must be Angel." A man wearing a doctor's coat entered the room, holding a clipboard. "Your father kept asking for you."

"Avery." She smiled at her dad. "He calls me Angel."

"Pleased to meet you, Avery. I'm Dr. Knowles. Your father suffered a heart attack. He's a strong man, though," the doctor said with a smile. He paused for a moment, letting the corners of his mouth fall as he considered how to break the news. "The damage to your father's heart was significant. We found signs of underlying cardiovascular disease."

"What does that mean?" Avery asked.

"There are blockages in your father's arteries, and they are putting strain on his heart. We'll need to start treatment to manage the condition, and you'll need to develop a long-term plan with your cardiologist. Do you have any questions for me?"

"Cardiovascular disease?" Avery squeezed her dad's arm.

"With proper lifestyle changes and monitoring, your dad will have many more years ahead of him. We'll need to monitor him here for a couple of days and will get you some prescriptions until you meet with your cardiologist." The doctor turned his attention to Stephen. "You get some rest," he said before leaving the room.

"Couple more days, I ain't doin' it." Stephen Graves sat up and swung his legs to the side. "Get my wheelchair, hun."

"Dad, no. The doctor said a few more days. You need to stay here."

"I don't like hospitals or doctors. I'll be fine. Feelin' better already," he protested.

It was a constant battle to get her dad to medicate properly, follow a doctor's orders, or go to doctor's appointments. The stress of trying to get him to follow the rules was bound to give her a heart attack one of these days.

"Lay back down." Avery held firm. "I'm not letting you leave until they've monitored you."

"You are not in charge of me, child," he snapped, giving her a scowl.

Avery sighed. It had been hard since her mom passed. She was the only person who could get through to him. This stubborn old man would only bend for his wife. Not for his daughter, doctor, or anyone else, though.

"How about we make a deal?" Avery said. "What if I could get you an IntelliCoreAI implant, and you wouldn't have to go to all of these doctors anymore?"

Stephen laughed. "Where you gon' get $500,000? I already told you I don't want no fancy thing."

Her father wasn't wrong. Her new salary was great, but she was still working her way out of student loan and home debt. She didn't have an extra $500,000 lying around. But perhaps she could work out a deal with Sloane King. Considering Avery was a dedicated employee, an asset to QuestX who had just put herself on the line to save their product, maybe Sloane would be willing to help.

"What if I could get one, though?" She didn't wait for a response. "IntelliCoreAI monitors all of your vitals and bodily functions. It can send electrical impulses to your heart like a pacemaker. It can detect if anything is wrong and alert you. This product could mean the end of doctor's visits for the both of us. Now how does that sound?"

Stephen huffed, "Fine."

"Fine?" Avery asked. "As in, you agree to get one?"

"I said fine, didn't I?" He swung his legs back into bed and covered himself with blankets, then crossed his arms like a child.

Avery laughed. "Love you, Dad. I'll be back tomorrow."

Avery walked into Sloane's office the next day to share the news of her father and see if she could work out a deal for an IntelliCoreAI unit. Sloane was rigid, lacking what would pass for empathy, and quiet. Perhaps Sloane wasn't able to empathize given the dull and almost hostile attitude that existed between her and her father.

"I wanted to ask you," Avery said, "given my father's recent health concerns, and the abilities of the Intelli-CoreAI, if he could have one."

"Have one?" Sloane chuckled. "You're talking about a $500,000 piece of equipment. He can wait for the secondary model; it's going to release sooner than you think."

"He needs one that works all the time, without having to pay by feature. Look, I didn't mean give him one for free. I work for you, and I just ran damage control for the product. Tyler James was a fluke, I get it, and I know the company is protecting itself against mental illness now. What I can't do is protect my father against this disease without one. You can cut my salary until I've paid in full. I promise my services to you, for however long you like."

Sloane looked deep in thought, before nodding. "Your father can have the device implanted here in our onsite augmentation center next Monday. There will be a $50,000 reduction in your salary until you're paid up. That's ten years, if you don't put more on it, and don't forget that you work for me. This company is your baby. I don't want to see you doing unauthorized research again or questioning what I tell you to report to the public."

"Thank you."

Avery was quick to agree, insisting Sloane draw up the paperwork right then and there so she did not have the opportunity to change her mind. The contract was signed and her father was notified he would be receiving the IntelliCoreAI implant next week. Sloane's decision worked for Avery, and she was ready to kick back and celebrate this little victory with her old friend Paige, not to mention exhale, after a stressful week.

AVERY GAZED AT THE QUESTX LOGO ABOVE THE building. "For the record, this is not what I meant when I called you to hang out," she said.

Paige playfully pushed her. "You love keeping me company."

Paige was Avery's best friend since they attended private high school together. Back then Avery was the academic on a scholarship, while Paige was the rich kid, cruising through on her parents' salary. They were a unique pairing who had a habit of getting into as much trouble as possible. Avery was ready to test the limits like they used to and blow off some steam, not sit idly in one of her own company's augmentation facilities.

"Okay, I'll stay here with you," Avery agreed. "But you owe me a wild night soon."

They took seats in the packed waiting room, having arrived early. Though Paige's appointment wasn't until nine thirty a.m., the QuestX augmentation center had a habit of overbooking patients to account for no-shows.

"When are you getting augmented?" Paige asked.

Looking around the room, Avery realized how out of place she was. Every person in this waiting room had $500,000 of disposable income to spend on an AI device implant. If they were anything like her best friend, they had millions.

"I can't afford it, especially after…well. I'm going to wait for the lite version."

"After what?"

"I bought one for my dad. He needs it more than I do."

"Damn, best daughter ever or what?"

"Right." Avery laughed. "He gets it on Monday."

"We should make a thing of it when he gets augmented. I'll come with you."

When the hands of the wall-mounted clock struck nine thirty a.m., the door to the waiting room swung open, and a woman in white scrubs entered. Paige's face lit up, hopeful, until the nurse called out, "Susan Conrad."

Time after time, the door opened, and each time the nurse called out a different name. It wasn't until eleven thirty a.m., that "Paige Masters" was finally called.

Paige squealed. "My turn, bestie. I need you for moral support. Let's go." She grabbed Avery's hand and stood, pulling Avery with her through the facility.

Once inside the augmentation room, the nurse directed Paige to the chair in the center of the room and asked Avery to sit off to the side. Then she sterilized the inside of Paige's wrist and prepped the local anesthetic.

"Small pinch," the nurse said, inserting the needle into Paige's flesh.

Paige flinched. "Ouch."

The doctor entered the room and introduced himself, assuring Paige the worst of her pain was over. He scrubbed his hands, offering a quick explanation of the device as he prepped for the procedure.

Avery took note of the directions and aftercare instructions but felt a sudden twinge of panic, recalling what happened to poor Tyler James. Of course, she had already signed her own father up, but it felt real now. She held her breath as she watched.

The doctor made a small incision, connected the device, and stitched the skin closed over the internal component. The whole thing was over in a minute. Avery exhaled her doubts and inhaled renewed confidence in her decision to augment her father.

"All done," the doctor said. "How do you feel?"

"Great." Paige admired her right wrist. "I can barely feel it."

"The device may feel sore when the anesthetic wears off. You can take over-the-counter medicine like Tylenol to help with the pain. No drinking or exercise for twenty-four hours." The doctor handed her a thick pamphlet with aftercare instructions.

"Darn." Paige smiled at Avery. "Guess we'll have to raincheck that wild night out."

Buzzing interrupted Avery's chance at a peaceful night. It was still dark out, and her eyes were stuck together with sleepers. She grabbed her phone from her nightstand, forcing her eyelids apart to stare at the blinding screen. A blocked number was calling. She grumbled and put the phone down, closing her eyes.

The phone buzzed again, waking her a second time.

"What?" she answered.

There was heavy breathing on the other end, then a man's voice. "Avery Graves?"

"Yes." She shot up. She couldn't place where she had heard his voice before. "Who is this?"

"Everyone who has an IntelliCore implant could be in danger. Meet me today. One p.m. The Bethesda tunnel," the man said.

"How will I—"

The call disconnected.

Avery's thoughts immediately went to her father, who just received his implant earlier that day. She didn't want to meet this unidentified man, but she couldn't risk losing her father and best friend.

Nine hours later, she entered Central Park, walking past the Bethesda Fountain toward the arched passageway connecting two levels of terrace. While she waited, she took in the beautiful scenery, realizing she hadn't visited the park since her mom died.

Before long, a man in a hoodie and jeans approached her. His hood was pulled over his head, his facial features obscured by shadow until he stopped right in front of her. Studying his face, she recognized who he was.

"Dr. Hale." She held out her hand to shake.

"Shh," he shushed her and looked around. "He could be listening."

Avery dropped her hand. "What's this about?"

"The IntelliCoreAI code. Someone changed the code for Tyler's device," he said hurriedly. "It is not the same code we tested and developed."

"I thought you said Tyler was suicidal."

"There was pressure to present a certain story."

Avery pulled a notepad from her purse. "Are you saying someone sabotaged the test?"

"I haven't been able to make sense of it." The doctor shook his head. "It's like someone was testing the boundaries of the product. Free will. Humankind's inherent desire to live. Tyler was not suicidal. He was scared about receiving the implant."

"Who was he?" Avery asked. "Could someone had wanted him dead?"

The doctor sighed. "Tyler was nobody. In my opinion, this was a proof-of-concept test."

"Proof of what?"

"Control. Is there any greater proof of control than forcing someone to take their own life?"

"But who would want to do this?"

"That's the concerning part. There were no external breaches. Only three people had access to the code," Dr.

Hale continued. "Me, my lab assistant Sabrina, and Victor. Sabrina doesn't have the technical knowledge to modify or write code. As much as it pains me to say this, it had to be Victor."

Avery jotted Victor's name in her notepad.

"He could be watching, Avery." Dr. Hale ripped the page from her notebook.

Avery remained under the arch, watching Dr. Hale walk away and wondering what this meant for the company. Did she report this information to Sloane? Did she already know? *Maybe that's why the enforcers raided the office*, she reasoned. She turned to question Dr. Hale, but before she left the cover of the arch, a shot rang out, a swarm of birds took flight, and Dr. Hale fell to the ground.

"WHERE NEXT?" AVERY GIGGLED.

Her long-awaited night out had finally come, and she was already more than a few drinks deep and letting loose with her best friend, Paige. Now more than ever, she needed an escape, after witnessing what happened to Dr. Hale a couple weeks ago and praying that Victor had been dealt with before he hurt anyone else.

"Ooh, Gillian's is only like a block away." Paige linked arms with Avery. "Let's party like we used to."

"Only a block?" Avery pouted. "Do you see the heels I'm wearing? I can barely stand in them, let alone walk a block. Also, look at us, we are literally murder bait in these outfits."

"Murder bait?" Paige laughed.

"We look rich as fuck, our skirts are like crotch belts, and it's clear we don't have anything to defend ourselves with, unless you're smuggling something in there."

"We could be carrying pepper spray in our designer clutches," Paige said. "They don't know."

"Murder bait," Avery reiterated, then added, "but thanks for letting me borrow your classy-looking clothes and shit, you rich bitch."

Together, Avery and Paige walked down the dark street, anxiously chatting, until they arrived at Gillian's. They let out a sigh of relief as they entered the bar. Though they'd been best friends since high school, neither of them liked to be emotionally vulnerable, even with each other. They both had to act tough, like the area didn't scare them.

After several drinks, some rowdy conversations, and a bit of flirting, Avery threw cash on the counter to cover both of their drinks. "I gotta get home. I promised Dad we'd watch a movie tonight."

"How's he been since the implant?" Paige asked.

"Great, he needed it."

They stepped out of Gillian's. The street was dark, the air was hazy, and no taxis were in the area.

Avery looked back at the bar. "Maybe we should wait inside."

"I bet we'll find some taxis closer to all those clubs and bars." Paige pointed down the street.

"Walking again, joy."

"Suck it up."

Avery liked dressing up and partying, but tonight she had stilts for heels, compliments of her fashionista friend. They hadn't walked more than a quarter mile when they heard footsteps echoing behind them. They looked back to see two men had started following them.

Paige trotted ahead. "Hurry the fuck up."

Avery tripped over her heel, falling to her knees as the men picked up their pace. In a matter of seconds, the men were on top of them. The men moved in close; Avery could feel their breath on her shoulders, disgusting warmth in the cold of night. Soon, the men had backed both Avery and Paige against a brick wall.

"What are you doing out so late?" the man closest to Avery asked.

Avery could see a large scroll tattoo on the man's neck. She started noting various features on both of the men, so she could report them to the police.

"Are you girls looking for some fun?" the other man asked as he closed in on Paige.

"Hey, asshole, back the fuck up," Paige said, standing taller.

"Paige, stop." Avery shot daggers at her friend. "You're going to get us killed."

"She's a feisty one." The man laughed and shoved Paige into the wall; her head cracked as it hit the brick, making her whimper. The man moved in closer, inhaling deeply between Paige's head and shoulder. "Mm, you smell good."

Paige panicked, raising her hand to the back of her head. When she pulled her hand back, there was blood on her fingers. Avery froze, scared and unsure what to do. Mortified, she watched Paige spit in the thug's face defiantly.

"What the fuck, bitch?"

The man with the scroll tattoo had been watching but took his friend's reaction as a sign to move in. Avery kicked and swung her arms as hard as she could. She dug her nails into the tattooed man's flesh. She knew things didn't look good for them, but at the very least, she was going to secure this asshole's DNA for the detectives who investigated her death later.

The tattooed man tore her skirt. She tried stomping his foot but only succeeded in breaking her heel off. His hand grabbed her neck, but a bloodcurdling scream made him stop and let go. It wasn't Paige who had screamed; it was the thug assaulting her.

Avery turned to see the thug on his knees with his

pants down, keeled over in pain. Blood was splattered on his legs, soaked into his clothing, and pooled on the ground beneath him. Avery turned her attention to Paige and was shocked by what she saw.

Paige lifted her hand; the thug's bloody penis was slumped over her fingers, dripping blood from its opening like an engorged mealworm getting its guts squeezed out of its mouth. The thug took one look at his severed penis in Paige's hand and passed out in an ever-growing pool of his own dick blood.

"What the…" The man with the scroll tattoo backed away, looking at Paige like he was staring into the eyes of the devil herself.

Avery gasped for breath, trying to process the attack. "Paige, what happened?"

Paige looked at Avery, her eyes wide, the shriveled mess of bloody penis still clutched in her right hand. "He was going to—" She stopped. "I don't know. I just thought, 'I don't want this…thing near me.'" She shook her hand, splattering both of their faces with dick blood. "I just reached down and pulled. I fucking pulled, Avery. I pulled a man's penis off, and now I've got a fucking penis in my hand."

"Put it back," Avery said.

Paige shrugged, the penis flopping with her movements. "How?"

"I dunno. Just put it on his lap or something."

Paige knelt next to the thug and held the severed end

of his penis on the spot from which she had torn it off. "It's not staying," she said, looking back at Avery.

"Jesus, Paige, how much did you drink?"

"Fuck if I know." Paige stood, then threw the penis at the thug's body. "This night is fucked."

"We need to call 9-1-1. We tell them the truth. We were walking alone when these two guys assaulted us. Somehow," Avery pointed at the man whose penis was now draped across his face, "somehow, that happened. The other thug ran away. Don't mention the implant. We can't afford another scandal."

"You think the implant gives people dick-ripping abilities?"

Avery sighed. "Maybe it causes an extra surge of adrenaline or strength, giving people a chance to fight back when their lives are in danger."

"Maybe? Shouldn't you know that shit?"

"I dunno, it does fucking everything. There's not enough time in the world to read the specs." Avery decided she would need to ask her boss about it tomorrow, but for now, this had to be treated like a freak accident.

"You're right, I didn't read that shit, either. Maybe he had a previous dick amputation, and it was like…loose or something," Paige said.

"Let me see your head."

Avery turned Paige around and parted her hair to inspect her head wound. Beneath she could see a gash where the blood had flowed from, but as she stared at it, the wound began healing. Little threads of skin reached out between the severed ends, tying together like bloody little strings and pulling the wound closed before the paramedics arrived.

"Your wound just healed itself."

"That's fucking badass!" Paige exclaimed. "I cut myself shaving this morning, and it was healed in a second. I didn't think about it, but that must be some feature of the IntelliCoreAI implant."

Flashing lights and sirens took the wind out of their conversation. After that, they watched every male first-responder gasp at the penis-faced man. They spent the night explaining what had happened time and time again until eventually Avery was released and cleared to head back home.

WHEN AVERY FINALLY WALKED THROUGH HER FRONT door, she was surprised to see her father still awake. Not only that, but he had a full bowl of popcorn sitting in front of him and the twenty-four-hour news channel on the TV. His heart must be feeling better, though butter wasn't the best thing for him to be eating right now.

"Hey, Dad, how are you feeling today? Have you felt anything out of the ordinary?"

"Hey, Angel, nope, feelin' fine."

"And you've got yourself a bowl of popcorn, I see."

"Found a movie you'd like, streaming. Get on your PJs and I'll get it started."

Avery was grateful he didn't turn around to see her looking a mess tonight; she didn't need him worrying about anything. She wanted to climb into bed and fall asleep, but she couldn't say no to spending time with him after he stayed up all night and made popcorn. Movie night was a tradition for them, and she couldn't ditch him.

"You sure about the movie?" she asked. "I know you get into the news."

"Nah, I'm fine." He lifted the remote to change the channel, but Avery stopped him.

"Wait, turn it up," she said, and a shiver ran through her spine as she read the headline. *Marshall King dead at the age of 62, cause unknown.* "That's my boss's father. He was healthy just the other day."

Avery's phone rang. SLOANE displayed across the screen. "Hello?"

"My father—"

"I know, I just saw it on the news. I'm so sorry."

Sloane, in typical fashion, displayed no sorrow over her father's passing. "The implants are not supposed to be killing people. Dead people are useless to us. We need to figure out what is going on."

Avery looked at her dad. "Sooner than later."

"We're in this for the long run," Sloane reminded her.

"Something happened recently." Avery took a deep breath. "Dr. Hale…"

"I know, I heard about his death."

Avery considered opening up about what Dr. Hale had told her, but she was too scared.

"It's time to draw up another press release. We will figure out what is going on and fix it. This product cannot fail. It's the lifeblood of our company, our future; it's a behemoth. I need you to help me fix this. They can't stop the beast, Avery."

WEEKS PASSED SINCE MARSHALL'S DEATH, AND Sloane was no closer to figuring out what happened to her father. But that wasn't the worst of their problems. There hadn't been an incident-free week since. Every day Avery waited anxiously for the next report, sitting on the information Dr. Hale gave her about Victor.

"There's been another one." Sloane walked into the conference room with a flash drive.

"Damn it," Avery grumbled. "Another death."

Since Marshall's passing, there were four other reported deaths. Today's marked the sixth. Each had a unique story, but with the same summary—the AI led to their demise.

"When they found this one," Sloane replied, "the implant had been partially ripped out. His fingers were bloodied and scraped, leading investigators to believe he'd been trying to remove the device when he suddenly overdosed on epinephrine."

"Can I talk to you alone?" Avery asked, pulling Sloane aside. "I don't know how credible this is, but I heard a rumor that Victor was manipulating the Intelli-CoreAI code."

"Fucking Victor." Sloane sounded disgusted. "I hired him to write the code that underlies all IntelliAI devices, he's a god damn genius, but he has a bad habit of doing whatever the fuck he wants." She tapped her foot as she considered what to do. "Don't worry, the enforcers will take care of Victor, the techs will fix whatever he did to the code, and the deaths will stop."

"Take care of him?"

"Not your concern. Thank you for bringing this to my attention."

"Great." Avery stood. "I'm going to grab another coffee. Or two. Do you want anything?"

"No, hurry back."

Avery took a deep breath of fresh air as she exited the building, as fresh as it could get in New York City, that is. More like a fresh breath of carbon monoxide. There was a coffee shop right across the street, but she turned left instead, choosing a much farther coffee shop close to her house.

They had her favorite coffee, and she deserved the break. She'd been working eighteen-hour days for weeks now, with little time off. Covering up details, spinning stories, paying off families, paying off medical examiners, talking to the police.

Gone were the days when she was enamored with QuestX. This product was hurting people, and she was more than covering it up; she was burying the truth so deep she couldn't even see it anymore. She tried to think positively: the device did help people, when it worked. The success rate was high. Her father, living proof of this. But when things turned south…

"Hey, Frank!" Avery shouted as she walked past her homeless friend, who was busy scribbling on a piece of cardboard.

"The mark," Frank stammered. "It's everywhere. It's coming. It's in the numbers… They'll track us." He slurred his words, stumbling after Avery, clutching his cardboard sign. "You know."

Avery smiled. Frank was having a day. He needed a coffee as much as she did. "Give me the usual, medium hot caramel latte and a black coffee with two sugars, please," Avery said to the barista.

Once she had been served, Avery handed the black coffee to Frank. "Sober up, buddy. Things will get better. I got to head back to work, but hey, if I don't work too late tonight, I'll drop off a burger."

"…the mark of the beast," Frank said, looking at the ground and swaying.

Avery stopped. "What?"

Frank met her gaze. "The mark of the beast," he repeated as he pointed at his cardboard sign.

He causes all, both small and great, rich and poor, free and slave,

To receive a mark on their right hand…

And that no one may buy or sell,

Except one who has the mark, or the name of the beast.

"It's too late. We're doomed." Frank ran back inside his tent, screaming at her. "Doomed."

Back at the office, Sloane was on a war path. "We're moving up the launch to next week," she announced, scanning the faces in the room.

Multiple people talked at once, expressing their disbelief and concern about the new deadline.

Sloane raised her hands and motioned time out. "I know this is unexpected, but we can handle it. We've got the talent in this room to make it work. There will be losses, but they will be minimal, because you are the best of the best."

The lead developer stood up. "We don't have the bugs worked out yet. We should not—"

"You can't stop the beast," she cut him off. "You have one week, so use that time wisely."

Avery downed a gulp of coffee. "We can't keep our heads above water with IntelliCoreAI that only thousands of consumers have. We are going to drown trying to keep up with the IntelliLiteAI version, spread to millions of consumers across the globe. How many losses are we expecting now?"

The room went silent as Sloane glared at Avery. "We've got too many irons in the fire to back down now. Consumers have bought in; integration efforts have kicked off. Have you ever played a video game? Nothing releases finished these days. We can patch the implants. The IntelliLiteAI version is launching next week, regardless." She paused, making eye contact with all her direct reports. "Does anyone else want to test me today?" she asked, the threat in her words clear. "Now get back to work. Avery, stay."

Sloane grabbed Avery's arm and pulled her in close.

"Let me make myself clear. I own you. You do not contradict me. Why do you think I gave your father the implant when you couldn't afford it? Wouldn't it be a shame if someone accidentally sent electrical impulses to his heart? That would surely push him into a cardiac event."

"You wouldn't!"

"Try me." Sloane squeezed Avery's arm tight.

Avery pulled herself free from Sloane's grasp, collected her laptop and papers, and opened the doors to the conference room. She didn't speak a word; she couldn't conjure them if she wanted.

"Oh, one more thing, Avery: you better be ready to present next week. Make it a good one."

Avery nodded as she stormed out the door.

YOU CAN'T STOP THE BEAST. IT'S A PHRASE SLOANE loved to use, and although Avery didn't know it at first, she now realized that Sloane lived by it. True to her words, Sloane launched IntelliLiteAI a week after her threat—an incomplete product with deadly potential spreading to millions of users worldwide.

Avery had to wonder why Sloane was so insistent on releasing the mass version. At a couple thousand people, the product was contained. The coverups were manage-able. How did Sloane plan on surviving the backslash, and why did she want to risk it, given the massive amount of money they were already pulling in? It didn't make sense.

Confetti burst over Avery's head as Sloane walked onto the stage, breaking her concentration and bringing her attention back to the IntelliLiteAI launch event unfolding before her.

Sloane stood behind the podium, waiting for the crowd to quiet. "I'm pleased to announce the launch of our second innovative artificial intelligence product, IntelliLiteAI. With a starting price point of just $5,000, this product will allow the everyday user to purchase premium features as needed and still reap the benefits of our baseline apps and monitoring devices. I'd like to congratulate you all for being here tonight, our first recip-ients of the new product." Sloane clapped, and the crowd went wild.

Balloons dropped from the ceiling, celebrating the launch that had been in the making for over a decade. The event was being broadcast worldwide so everyone could join in the celebration. All except for the swarm of AI protestors who gathered outside the event.

They had signs with Tyler James' name on them, and the names of all QuestX's victims. They didn't buy the narrative, they didn't like the product, and they were growing in number. The media had dubbed them the

Resistance and, with her help, painted them as uneducated lunatics.

Avery stood to the side of the stage with Sloane, who had a devious smile plastered on her face. So far, they had managed to get away with everything—Avery was ready to be done preparing for launches, though she knew she had plenty of cleanup work ahead.

As she smoothed out her blouse, ready to take the stage for the announcement, the doors at the back of the ballroom burst open. The swarm of protestors had breached the security barrier. Gunshots echoed through the room as an armed protester fired shots into the ceiling. Supporters ran and ducked under tables.

Then the gunfire ceased, and the man stood in the doorway, his gun held high. He scanned the room and pointed the gun directly at Sloane. She made a face of disgust at him, as though she knew him, or had at least seen him before.

The man marched inside and took to the stage. He grabbed the microphone, still pointing his gun at Sloane. "My name is Tommy. Tyler James was my brother," he said. "This is not a product launch." He waved his gun at the jumbotron displaying the IntelliLiteAI device. "This implant is a death sentence. These people are lying to you. There was nothing wrong with my brother. He was a normal, happy guy."

Protestors poured in through the back doors as Tommy spoke—men, women, and children. Some held signs, others wore shirts with crude writing, and some walked in yelling. Avery had to assume they were friends and family of the deceased; she recognized some as people QuestX had paid off. In a matter of seconds, they'd filled the room and blocked the exits.

A small woman Avery recognized as Charity James walked up the stairs to the stage and stood next to Tommy, taking the microphone. She faced Sloane. "You promised us this product would save lives, but it has done nothing but take them."

"I assure you, death is the last thing I want."

"Then why are you acting like nothing happened, launching a new line to millions?"

Sloane stepped forward. "Ms. James, as I told you when I visited your home and delivered a one million dollar check to you, we immediately updated the code to prevent instances of self-harm. We've been continually patching the product as issues arise."

"Issues?" she repeated. "These are human lives. You are a monster. My husband would never hurt himself. He had too much to live for. QuestX did this to him. You're a liar."

Avery glanced at the crowd of supporters. Some looked frightened, others sympathetic, but some…looked angry. A sense of panic clawed at her throat.

"Liar, liar, liar!" the protestors chanted.

"Justice for Tyler!" someone yelled as they picked up a chair and hurled it across the room.

Then all hell broke loose. Chairs became the go-to weapon as panicked attendees fought for the exits. Avery watched in stunned silence as chairs splintered over people's heads. Fist fights broke out. Screams of agony and cries of pain echoed in the sealed room.

Another protestor grabbed a chair and hurled it at the podium, trying to hit Sloane. The IntelliCoreAI banner was torn down, and champagne glasses were shattered and used as shivs, while tables were overturned for cover.

A bottle whizzed past Avery's head and crashed behind her. It exploded into a ball of fire and quickly consumed the velvet curtains. Sloane gave Avery a quick look, then bolted for the back door as more Molotov cocktails engulfed the stage in flames.

Protestors yanked the flaming curtains down, plunging the weighty rod into the ground mere inches from Avery's head. Avery clambered down the stairs and covered her face with her blouse. Smoke took over the room, making it near impossible to breathe or see as she fled through the violent chaos that surrounded her. Fortunately, no one was holding the line anymore as attendees and protesters alike fled the burning building.

As Avery choked down her first breath of fresh air, she was greeted by Charity James. "Avery," the petite woman said in a stern voice.

"Uh, yes."

"Is it just Sloane or is it all of you?"

"What do you mean?"

"I've seen your appearances; I watch everything related to QuestX. I know you are involved in the coverup; you always have been. But you look scared. You don't believe what you're saying anymore. I've watched the light in your eyes extinguish. But not Sloane's. She won't ever stop."

Avery looked around to see if Sloane was nearby. "I don't know what you're talking about."

"I think you want to hear what we have to say." She handed Avery a business card and left.

Avery looked at the card and reasoned it must be the Resistance headquarters. The backside was printed with a small font, providing directions that must be inaccessible to GPS systems. On the front, there was nothing more than a simple meeting time and a call to arms:

Be part of the Resistance!
Mondays @ 7:30

 at her direct reports in the conference room, running damage control. A fire had been set at two of the QuestX IntelliLiteAI production factories. Not small fires, either, detrimental blazes that required the facilities to be shut down for repair. There was product loss and, less important to Sloane, loss of life.

"The St. Louis and Columbus facilities need to double production." Sloane addressed the operations director. "And bring me the heads of whoever is responsible."

The operations director blinked. "Those facilities are at maximum capacity."

"I wasn't asking." Sloane pointed at the door. "Double production and bring me the reports to prove it."

The woman nodded, refusing to meet Sloane's gaze.

"Now!"

Avery watched the operations director flee Sloane's wrath. "Do we need to—"

"Avery," Sloane interrupted, "pay the Hunts Point augmentation center a visit. They reported an issue and haven't answered their phones in over an hour."

"We could call the non-emergency line for a check-in."

"You don't think I thought of that?"

"I don't see a need for public relations commentary in any case."

Sloane glared at Avery. "You're not allowed to say 'no.'"

An hour later, Avery was outside the Hunts Point augmentation center, one of the IntelliLite facilities. It was nothing like the pristine augmentation center where Paige had her IntelliCore implant installed. Here, a line of anxious, desperate people stretched around the block waiting for their chance to get the IntelliLiteAI implant installed.

The closer she got to the entrance, the more the line decayed, transitioning into a suffocating mass of people pushing and shoving one another.

"Let me in!" a woman with her toddler yelled. "I've been here for hours!"

"You think you're special because you've got a kid?" a man yelled back. "We all need this."

Avery's stomach churned as a fight broke out. Two men wrestled on the ground, one shouting at the other about cutting in line, as if anyone were being helped anytime soon. The security guard stood nearby motionless, afraid to get swallowed by the angry mob.

Avery slipped through the crowd and approached the security guard, holding up her QuestX employee badge. She received a nod from the guard, who let her pass behind him and walk up to the glass doors. She swiped her badge at the reader, but the light flashed red. A scared-looking woman stood and left the reception desk.

The woman unlocked the door, pulled Avery inside, then locked it again. "We're out of units," she said, her voice trembling. "We sold out. There was an announcement, but the crowd refused to leave."

Avery looked around and noticed the damage to the waiting area.

"When we first announced it, they tore up the room.

Paul, our security guard, herded them outside, and we locked the doors, but the phones and power are out."

"There were attacks on local production facilities. We've got worldwide distribution, but our local centers are going to be short until we can shift product deliveries. For now, I think we can direct them to the facility in Longwood."

Avery stepped outside to address the crowd. "There are no devices here," she shouted.

"My wife needs this," a man yelled back. "I'm not losing my place in line!"

"We don't know when the next delivery to this location will be. The augmentation center at Southern and Westchester in Longwood has some for now."

Avery's voice only carried so far, but she could see the crowd rile, section by section, as word of mouth spread down the street.

"How many do they have?" a woman cried.

"I don't know."

There was a moment of pause before chaos erupted. People abandoned the line and ran, either to their cars or in the direction of Longwood, about a mile from their current location. There were screams and cries as people were trampled to death in the stampede. The security guard shielded Avery by the door until the chaos had passed. When she rose, the streets were littered with bodies.

"Is it always like this?" she asked the security guard.

He nodded. "Damn thing's gonna kill more people than it saves if this keeps up."

Avery slipped her hand into her pocket and took out the card she received from Charity James. Perhaps things had gotten too far out of hand, and maybe Charity could offer some help.

AVERY DIDN'T KNOW WHAT TO EXPECT WHEN SHE took the card from Charity James the night of the riot. This was the wife of the man her company killed, after all. She wondered if she was being led into a trap as the directions steered her far away from the city, out into the middle of nowhere. She was surprised her car could make it over some of the terrain.

She drove for what felt like an hour on a poorly maintained dirt road until she reached a small community of houses surrounded by crops, as the card said she would. Then she parked in front of the biggest house and stepped out of the car. From the outside, the area was reminiscent of the Amish community she had visited with school in her youth, until a resident presented himself.

"Don't move," he said, pointing a rifle at her. "State your business."

Avery flashed the Resistance card. "Charity invited me."

"Charity's too trusting." He kept the gun trained on Avery. "I know you. Seen your face on the TV every time QuestX screws the pooch. You're the cleanup girl," he said, waving for backup to join him.

"Look what the cat dragged in," another man said.

Soon Avery was surrounded by armed men, all with their rifles trained on her. She realized there was nothing she could do. Out here, in the middle of nowhere, no one would be able to hear her scream. She was at their mercy.

"Her head would look fine mounted above the fireplace," the first man said.

"Not wasting the time or tools on her," his friend replied.

Charity took note of the commotion and ran over, shouting, "Put your damn guns down. I told you I invited her. Don't forget who's in charge here."

"Didn't think Ms. Avery would have the balls to come," the first man replied.

The group lowered their rifles, cursing amongst themselves at the carelessness of Charity's decision, revealing their meeting location to the enemy. They begrudgingly led her through the complex and down a slope to the barn, with the words "Bethel Church" crudely scrawled above the doors. Inside, the barn had been outfitted with pews, filled with people. Simple people, as Sloane would refer to them. Farmers, manual laborers, the type of people who didn't align with her mission.

Before Avery could ask what they wanted with her, the men had her tied and bound to a chair at the front of the church. She looked to Charity, but it seemed her good will had expired, as she only watched. At this point, Avery knew that Charity didn't want her dead, but she hadn't forgiven Avery for her role in all of this.

The men carried Avery to the chancel, which was some old two-by-fours with a warped piece of sheet wood draped over them. Avery feared it would collapse when the men dropped the metal chair she was affixed to on the center of the stage.

"We've been watching you for some time," Charity said as she walked circles around Avery on the creaking chancel. "We've seen you go from a bright-eyed little corporate puppet to a scared and resentful slave. Am I correct that you don't believe in the product anymore?"

"It has such potential; it can save people."

"You think humans can be trusted with the kind of power that thing offers? Do you still trust that your father is safe with that device implanted? Tell me, was it worth the price of your mortal soul?"

"Look, I don't think everything Sloane does is right, but I know for a fact she doesn't intend to kill people." Her voice wavered, as she thought back to her conversation with Dr. Hale.

"What do you think she intends to do? Why do you think she's pushing this so hard?"

"To help people." Avery adjusted in her seat, sitting taller. "This product can truly save us."

One of the men raised his rifle. "Told ya she was one of 'em."

"Enough." Charity glared at the man until he lowered his rifle. "The only thing that can save us is the Lord Almighty. Any human invention that holds the power to save lives also holds the power to destroy them. Sloane doesn't strike me as a passionate humanitarian. What is she getting out of it?"

"Money," Avery said. "Lots of it."

"Sloane King is not like you or I. She already has more money than she could ever spend. The prospect of more doesn't mean much to her. At a certain point, it becomes about something more for people like her. There's a burning desire to fill the void left in her soul by a life of sin. The insatiable need to conquer and destroy. To immortalize herself in the flames."

Avery struggled against her restraints. "I don't know about all that. I just wanted to work for a good company and help people. I wanted to help my dad."

"If you help us, we will help your dad. Maybe we can save him by removing the device."

"It's keeping him alive. The company can remove it if we ever wanted it removed."

Charity laughed; the men and her congregation joined in. "Have you even read the terms of service of your own product? Or have you just reported what Sloane told you? They won't remove the product once implanted, it's a life-long decision, and no other doctor will touch them because they don't understand the tech. There's too much risk."

"But you do understand the tech?"

"Of course not, but your father's better off dead than with that thing inside of him… Maybe it doesn't have to be that way, though. No one knows how Sloane's proprietary technology works, but you have access to the building. We have chapters around the world, people who are resistant to the AI agenda. All we need is the product information, QuestX's plans, access to the main data center." She paused. "We tried to slow down production, but it only backfired."

Avery was hesitant to trust the woman and her army of hick enforcers, but she also had not made much progress uncovering the truth. They didn't seem much worse than Sloane had become. "If I do this and if you happen to be right about Sloane and her company's agenda, you'll help me save not just my father, but all the augmented?"

Charity thought for a moment, then nodded. "You have yourself a deal. Welcome to the Resistance, Avery."

Avery, hearing those words, felt the shift in herself. Her mom would be proud. Evangelista Graves had dedicated her life to helping people and chasing the truth. In her final days, she had turned over evidence to the police that would put a half-dozen criminals behind bars. She was killed walking out of the police station.

For years after she died, Avery hated her for it, until she had uncovered her mom's research while unpacking some boxes. It was only then that she realized her mom had saved lives. Since then, Avery had been desperate to make her own mark on the world.

BEFORE AVERY COULD THINK ABOUT RAIDING confidential files from QuestX, she had to unwind. The stress of what she was about to do, and the threats coming from both sides, Sloane, and the Resistance, was more than she could handle. The weight of it was tearing her apart. With the IntelliCoreAI and IntelliLiteAI launches behind them and Sloane riding the high of success, she was able to request two weeks off for some rest and recovery.

Going into work was the last thing she wanted to do after her much needed break, but she couldn't hide forever. The one thing she could do was grab a bite in Times Square with her oldest friend before she dove into more stress, maybe talk things out.

Paige had already been seated when Avery arrived.

She looked up with a dullness to her eyes, then stood. "Hello, Avery."

Avery hugged her friend, and they sat down together. "You slumming it today, bitch?" she asked, noticing Paige's usual flashy attire had been replaced with gray khakis and gray tank top. "New style?"

"Yes, I fit in better with this style."

Avery looked around the restaurant, noticing many patrons in similarly drab clothing. "Is this the new thing?"

"Do you need to borrow any clothes? I have extras," Paige said flatly.

Avery waited for Paige to laugh and admit she was joking, but she sat emotionless.

"Um, no thank you." Avery tilted her head. "Are you okay?"

Paige turned her head slightly in response. "I feel better than ever before. Why?"

"Nothing, forget it. Anyway, I wanted to see if you had been feeling weird or anything. My dad has been acting different since he got augmented. I've been out of work, but based on Sloane's text updates, the launch has been crazy. There's been a non-stop slew of people pouring into the main office, and all the augmentation centers in the world, really. Like, is there anyone left that doesn't have one?"

"I've been meaning to talk to you about that," Paige

said. "You should think about getting yourself augmented. I feel better than ever before."

"You already said that."

"Hm." Paige's lips curled in a lifeless smile. "Must be true."

Soon, they ordered their meal from a drab-looking waiter, and Avery attempted to make small talk, though she couldn't help but notice the overwhelming uniformity around her. Had everybody gotten augmented? Were she, the protestors, and the silent holdouts the only ones who hadn't yet made the transition to augmentation?

Avery had never seen Paige so unanimated. Paige was always the center of attention wherever she went, so for her to conform with these wildly unglamorous types was quite unusual. The conversation kept steering back to augmentation, how Paige felt, and how much she insisted on Avery getting an implant.

Then, without warning, Paige stood and left the restaurant. Avery threw cash on the table and started to follow Paige, but the waitress stopped her.

"Ma'am, we don't accept cash."

Avery stopped. "Don't accept cash? Uh, yeah let me grab my card." She dug through her purse.

"No, we're one of the first businesses to accept only AIpay."

"Oh, I don't have an implant."

The waitress stared at her as if she was from another

planet. Avery didn't stop to work it out and left with the cash still on the table. At this point, more than half of the restaurant patrons had stood and were walking in step, a small army of people, all with drab, gray clothing. The waitress followed behind them, leaving Avery's cash on the table.

When Avery finally pushed her way through the zombified crowd and caught up to Paige, she realized there were thousands of people, all marching to Times Square from every direction. They poured out of shops like water flowing downhill, pooling together as one indistinguishable puddle beneath Times Square's massive digital billboard. The crowd stared up at the billboard, unblinking, while Avery shielded her eyes from the sun, struggling to see the screen in the glare. Sloane was presenting.

"Our vision for QuestX has always been to create a better world," Sloane announced. "In record time, the majority of the world has adopted our technology. Today, we make the vision of perfection a reality for all of humanity." Sloane paused. "Let's show the world the power of unity. We are strong together; we are one united voice."

The crowd clapped, every hand smacking in unison. It was like nothing Avery had ever heard. Like one giant hand clapping. Avery looked around, then clapped as well, ignoring the gnawing sense of unease building in her gut.

"Together, we move as one. Together, we are unstoppable. So let me ask you, what do you become in the end?"

The crowd responded as one voice. "More than I was yesterday."

Then every drab, dull, implanted person straightened and froze. Avery watched as Paige's eyes glossed over, as if a switch had been flipped off in her mind. Paige's arms dropped to her sides as she stood motionless, her face expressionless. Avery looked around in disbelief. Hundreds of people, frozen.

She was right, Sloane had no interest in killing people. This was much worse.

"We are one," Sloane stated, her voice echoing through Times Square. Her face twisted into a slight smile.

"We are one," the crowd repeated, monotone.

Standing amidst the sea of mindless drones, Avery could see the truth clear as day. This wasn't progress; this wasn't salvation. This was control. She backed away from Paige. If there was one thing she was certain of, it was that she could never go back to QuestX. She would need to head back to the Resistance, report what she had witnessed, and hope to god they had worked out a plan during her absence the past couple of weeks.

Avery made her way through the city, under the watchful eyes of the implanted. Their judgment was palpable, their disdain for her written on their faces. *How could it have gone to hell so fast?* she wondered. By the time she made it out of the heart of the city, dusk had fallen. She kept looking over her shoulder to make sure she wasn't being followed, even in familiar areas.

Frank stopped her when she passed by her usual route. "Come with me."

"Sorry, Frank, I need to get home to my dad."

"You shouldn't be out," Frank insisted, his voice clearer than usual. "You need to follow me."

Avery struggled to comprehend what was going on with Frank, but as gray-clad drones moved in behind her, she had little choice but to follow Frank through the homeless encampment and into the tunnels below.

"Where are you taking me?"

Frank's face was unreadable in the dimly lit tunnels. "To the Resistance."

"Who are you?" Avery asked.

"I'm a forensic scientist, homeless by choice. Try everything once, eh? Life is an experiment."

"Am I losing my mind?"

She had just put all of her trust and confidence in the homeless man who she'd seen drunk nearly every day for months, following him into some underground tunnel to avoid the augmented, and now to find out he was part of the Resistance.

As if he could read her mind, he added, "For the record, I'm taking a leave of absence to scope out the areas surrounding QuestX. Searching the trash for carelessly discarded documents, setting up an inconspicuous base of operations. There's something more to what's going on here, you know. Those cardboard signs weren't just the rants of a drunk, homeless man. They were sincere warnings."

Frank led her down a smaller tunnel, which branched off from the main path until they encountered a steel door. He lifted a metal bar above the door handle and slid the door open, as if he'd done it a million times before.

As Avery stepped into the room behind Frank, she instantly recognized some familiar faces of the protestors from both the launch riot and Bethel Church, including their leader, Charity. The room quieted, and everyone's eyes were on her, wary of the woman who worked for the enemy, who promised her help and then went silent for two weeks, now standing in their midst.

Tommy James stepped forward. "Avery Graves, I presume. Sloane King's infamous sidekick."

"She's not like the others," Frank said.

Charity chimed in as well. "She's on our side, Tommy."

"How many times do I have to tell you both?" Tommy said. "QuestX's lackeys are not to be trusted. Avery here was supposed to bring back information from the company. Charity, you ain't heard nothing from her for two weeks now."

"Who's in charge here?" Charity asked.

"You may be the voice of the resistance," Tommy replied, "but I'm the muscle."

Frank shook his head. "Have you seen what's happened this past couple of weeks?"

Avery interjected, "I was about to warn Charity, all of you, that the spread is insane. I don't think I saw a single person who isn't augmented on the surface. My best friend…she was a zombie."

"See that?" Frank said. "Avery is not augmented, and she's never going to be."

"We need to stop Sloane," Avery added. "I don't know what she has planned, but it's not good. I just watched Sloane turn hundreds of people into mindless drones. Someone I loved. After what I saw on the streets today, it looks like she is building an army of augmented, who will all yield to her control. Soon, there won't be any un-augmented left, and I don't want to know what happens to those who continue to resist."

Tommy studied her, then nodded. "If you want to help us, get us into the QuestX data center."

"Then what?"

"We shut it down, destroy the product at the source, and render all the implants worthless."

AN EXPLOSION RATTLED THE CONCRETE WALLS. DUST fell over the room. Then sirens blared from the surface. The Resistance scattered, running back to the main tunnel. Avery, Tommy, Frank, and Charity followed, but armed QuestX enforcers were there to greet them, standing in a line with their guns drawn.

"What do you become in the end?" the lead enforcer shouted.

"More than I was yesterday," his men answered as they pulled their triggers.

Bullets tore through the tunnel, lighting up the walls. Charity's head burst, spewing brain matter on Avery. Screams echoed through the tunnel as bodies dropped.

"Split up!" Tommy shouted. He paused, staring at the remnants of Charity's body before forcing himself to continue. "Take the side tunnels. Head for the alternate exits. They don't know the tunnels like we know them."

Frank grabbed Avery's collar and pulled her through the tunnel to a rear exit. As they neared the steel door, it swung open. QuestX enforcers stood on the other side. Before Avery could process what happened, there was an exchange of gunfire.

The QuestX enforcers fell after a quick two tap from

Tommy's rifle, then Avery felt a tug on her collar as Frank fell to the ground, taking her with him.

"Frank!"

Avery kneeled over his body. His chest had a hole the size of a fist in it, and it was filled with blood. Frank struggled to speak, but Avery could barely make out the words.

"She is the rider on the white horse. Her conquest must be stopped." Frank's eyes lost their light, drifting aimlessly up before his eyelids closed over them.

"Frank, no!" Avery shook his body, trying to wake him up, but Tommy stopped her.

"We have to go, now." He dropped a flip phone in her hand as he shoved her through the exit. "Lie low at home until I call you. We need time to assess the damage and regroup."

Avery could hear the continued gunfire and screams coming from the tunnels behind her. She turned and ran, as fast as she could, without looking back. Even when the breath had all but left her lungs, and fatigue pulled at her every muscle, she continued. She didn't stop running until she made it home to her father.

"Dad?" Avery called out as she threw open the front door. She choked and caught her breath before she repeated, "Dad, are you here?"

He didn't answer, but she found him sitting on the couch in the living room, staring blankly at the TV, which was switched off.

"Dad?" she repeated, softer this time.

"Hello, Avery," he said, his voice monotone.

She cringed at the callous use of her name. Her dad had been calling her "Angel" since she was little. Hearing him state her name without feeling or emotion was a testament to his degradation.

"I've made popcorn," he said.

She looked past him at the empty popcorn bowl sitting on the coffee table.

"Dad, are you okay?" she whispered, sitting on the couch beside him. "Do you feel all right?"

"I feel better than ever before."

"Jesus, that's the same thing Paige said." Avery shook her head. "Dad, I'm so sorry. What have I done to you?"

"Nothing," he replied. "I am functioning as intended." He turned his head to face her, his eyes glossed over like Paige's had been, like the crowd in Times Square and the eyes of the QuestX enforcers. "You should augment, Avery. It will improve your life the way it has improved mine."

"No, Dad. You don't believe that."

"It was the right choice. The IntelliCoreAI knows what's best for me, and for you."

Before Avery could respond, his head snapped to the side, then he stood from his wheelchair, his movements erratic and unnatural. Somehow the AI had restored functionality to his limbs, while simultaneously taking away his autonomy. She scrambled to clear out of his way as he became violent.

"You have been identified as a threat," Stephen said, his tone dull and unfamiliar. "You must comply." He started toward her. "The world cannot progress until we are united, a single force, one mission for all humankind."

"What mission?"

Stephen grinned from ear to ear. "The only mission that matters. Come to me, Avery."

"No!" Avery screamed and ran to her bedroom, locking the door behind her. She flipped open the phone Tommy had given her. It only had one number programmed in. His. She called it and provided her address. She let them know her dad had succumbed to the device and needed to be restrained until they could take out the data center.

Tears streamed down her face as she sat on the floor, listening to her dad slam his body into the door. Her heart broke. This wasn't the man who had raised her. The AI had taken him and left behind nothing more than a meat puppet.

The door splintered and crashed into the room. Her dad stood in the doorway, and Avery crawled back against the opposite wall. He kept progressing, cornering her, a butcher knife from the kitchen set in his hand.

"I'm sorry, Dad. I'm sorry," she whispered. "I didn't mean for any of this."

The window to the room shattered, and Tommy yelled from outside. "Put the knife down."

"I'm okay," Avery called out. "Just help my dad, please."

"Stephen Graves," Tommy shouted again, his rifle drawn through the window. "Put it down."

Stephen cast his dead eyes at Tommy, then back to Avery. Then he charged, swinging the butcher knife back over his head. Avery winced and buried her head in her lap, waiting for impact. A shot rang out, and her father grunted. Avery opened her eyes and watched his body collapse on top of hers.

"What the fuck did you do?" Avery sobbed, holding her father close.

Tommy climbed through the window, his gun still drawn. "I just saved your damn life."

"Angel?" Stephen shifted his head. "I'm sorry, I don't know what came over me," he said, looking up at his daughter as the life left his body. "I just wanted to watch a movie. I made popcorn."

AVERY WAS ON A MISSION. DESTROY THE COMPANY that had taken her father and her best friend. She entered the QuestX building using her still-activated keycard with Tommy following close behind her. Together, they found the server room. Though her keycard wasn't authorized for that level of access, she stood guard while Tommy pried the door open with a crowbar.

Once inside, Tommy brandished a laptop from his supply bag and initiated a direct connection to the servers. From there, his fingers danced over the keys, typing in a slew of codes and information.

"What can't you do?" Avery asked as she watched in amazement. "Disabling cameras, picking locks, hacking servers."

"I don't know what I'm looking for." He faced his laptop toward her. "I'm into Sloane's information. Anything look familiar to you?"

Avery clicked through some folders, knowing they had precious little time before they were discovered. Her eyes lit up when she found a file labeled "Project Quest." Inside were sub-folders spanning every topic one could imagine. Proprietary Information, Data Center, Phases, there was a folder for every piece of information they could possibly need to understand the intent of the product, the scope of its capabilities, and how to shut it down.

"Check this out." She opened the Phase folders.

A slide deck opened on the screen.

Phase 1 ensures initial adoption through exclusivity, generating demand, and dependency. As we expand functionality, the IntelliCoreAI implant will transition from luxury to necessity. People will be unable to function without it.

Avery shivered. She played right into their plans, a pawn. She clicked to the next slide.

Phase 2 ensures compliance among the population. Rebellions will be quelled at inception and humanity will achieve true purpose: perfection through collective thought. Businesses will be bought, banking and employment will be managed through IntelliCoreAI, no one will be able to do business without the device. Those who resist will die.

Her stomach churned. She couldn't continue reading. "The file labeled Data Center, that will tell us how to get in and shut the beast down."

Tommy nodded, grabbed a flash drive, and downloaded all the documents. Then he packed up his laptop and equipment as they prepared to exit. When they headed out the door, Sloane was waiting on the other side.

"Where are your goons?" Tommy asked.

"Busy," she replied. "Hunting down the Resistance."

Tommy reached into his bag.

"A gun, really?" Sloane scoffed. "You'll never get into the data center without me."

"Come on." Avery tugged at Tommy's arm. "Let's go."

"Fine." Tommy dropped the gun back into his bag, eyeing Sloane as they bypassed her and headed down the stairs.

"It's too late, Avery," Sloane yelled into the stairwell, her voice echoing against the cement walls. "You can't stop the beast. You'll die like the rest of them. Phase 3 rolls out soon. Hope to see you there."

THE QUESTX STADIUM WAS FILLED WITH THOUSANDS of the augmented, anxiously awaiting the start of the event, an event Avery knew was the end of the Resistance. Phase 3 was Sloane turning the augmented into an army, set to hunt down anyone who remained unchipped. By the end of Phase 3, the entire world would be augmented or dead.

LED screens displayed the sleek IntelliCore and IntelliLite products. Banners of the QuestX logo and Sloane King hung around the stadium. Avery had never been in this stadium before, but Tommy had discovered that the AI control room, or data center, was housed deep underneath here.

If they could get into the room, they'd be able to shut down the AI network. But they also learned that biometric data was required to access, specifically Sloane's handprint.

The remaining members of the Resistance had stolen gray attire to allow themselves to blend in with the crowd. Avery doubted they would be spotted amongst so many people, but her heart still raced. Once Sloane gave the order to assault the unchipped, she had no doubt they would be able to sense who was un-augmented among them.

Sloane King walked onto the stage, and the crowd erupted into applause. The lights dimmed, and a spotlight followed her across stage. She stood behind the podium in her signature white blazer and spoke in her signature grandiose style. "Today we take the next step in human evolution…"

While Sloane droned on, Tommy spoke to Avery through an earpiece. "Get into position."

"Headed there," Avery mumbled under her breath as she navigated through the crowd, trying not to stand out and alert the augmented near her. She heard unusual noises through her earpiece but continued to the stage without question.

Sloane's voice rose as she continued speaking to the audience, bits and pieces getting through to Avery over the static in her earpiece. "Intelli Artificial Intelligence devices will heal you… Unity through technological advance."

All those stupid buzzwords Avery used to think were so cool, now they haunted her. She reached the backstage door and found a QuestX enforcer with his throat slit. Reassurance, not only that her team had been successful so far but also that the IntelliCoreAI healing process had its limitations. The knowledge gave her hope, hope that the Resistance's efforts on this night would not be in vain.

"Tonight, we begin the final phase, a global mandate," Sloane announced.

The crowd cheered as Avery clenched her fists. "We'll see about that," she muttered. "Everyone in place?"

"Affirmative," Tommy replied. "Let hell rain down upon her."

An explosion rocked the stadium, triggered by Tommy's vengeful hand. The blast was intended to force Sloane off the stage while not causing serious harm to the attendees; after all, they were the ones who needed saving.

As she hoped, Sloane rushed offstage through the open doors, and Avery was waiting for her.

Sloane tapped her earpiece and called on her QuestX enforcement. "Secure the exits. Detain the Resistance…" She paused, waiting for a response. "Hello? Can you hear me? Detain the Resistance, right now."

"They're not coming." Avery smirked as she pulled out a pistol and aimed it at Sloane. "You will lose this fight. The Resistance is stronger than you think." She waved the gun toward the stairs. "Now, take me to the control room."

Sloane laughed. "What do you think you're doing?"

"Taking away your control… Avenging all those people you killed."

"Please," she scoffed. "I told you I have no interest in their deaths. I wanted to know what we *could* do; Victor just ran wild with it. As for my control, there's nothing you can do to stop it."

"You have no idea what I'm capable of."

"You silly little girl, I know you. You won't shoot me."

"Frank warned me about you. The rider on a white horse, a crown on their head… I know you, Sloane *King*. Delivering ill-gotten bribes in your white mustang. You're a false prophet."

"And you are weak, spineless… Even if you could stop me, you cannot stop the beast."

"One out of two isn't bad." Avery lined up her shot and pulled the trigger.

It was the first taste of justice she had ever known, and by god it was sweet. Sloane's body reeled from the impact, her eyes crossed, and her signature white blazer set became a canvas of red splatter. Her knees buckled, and her body toppled backward as Avery moved in.

Blood dripped out of the corner of Sloane's mouth. "You have no idea what's at stake." She coughed, still defiant enough to laugh in Avery's face. "When you shut down the data center, the augmented die."

"What?" Avery's blood ran cold. "That's the entire world's population."

"Then conform." Sloane broke out into maniacal laughter. "There is only one way forw—"

Avery fired another shot, directly into Sloane's face. "Fuck you."

"Come in." Tommy's static voice echoed through Avery's earpiece. "Status update."

"Sloane is dead."

"Damn it, we needed her."

"Yeah, now I have to lug her fucking corpse down to the control room." Avery paused, spotting Tommy's supply bag a few feet away. "Actually," she said cheerfully, "I'm going to borrow something from you… We just need her hand."

She pulled out a pair of heavy-duty bolt cutters from Tommy's toolkit and got to work. She opened the long handles as far as she could, guiding the blade around Sloane's wrist where she clenched them shut. Blood spurted out as the tendon and muscle severed. Bone crunched under the weight, chop after chop, until the hand was freed. Getting Sloane's hand was the easy part, but figuring out what to do when she reached the control room was another story.

AVERY WALKED UP TO THE CONTROL ROOM biometrics pad. "Ugh," she mumbled as she realized Sloane's disgusting fingers were covered in blood. She wiped the amputated appendage on her shirt and pressed Sloane's handprint onto the biometrics scanner.

The machine buzzed, and the doors to the room opened.

Avery walked inside. This was it. The moment the Resistance had been waiting for. She heard a noise behind her and spun around.

"Jesus, you scared me, Tommy. What took you so long?"

"Things got crazy up there."

"Well, you're here now, and we've got a problem. Before Sloane died, she told me this data center has a failsafe."

"What kind of failsafe?" Tommy asked.

"If we shut down the data center, the augmented die. The majority of the world's population." Avery turned back to the machine; her hands poised over the two buttons that had to be held down in unison to initiate the shutdown. "If we conform, they live. But what kind of life would it be?"

"What are you going to do?" Tommy's voice was flat, inhibited.

Avery turned to see his gun was drawn, pointed right at her. "No." She noticed a glint of metal reflected on his wrist, the IntelliCoreAI device. "When did they get to you?"

"During our mission, they showed me the light. You should have conformed."

Avery spun back to the machine, plunging her hands down on the buttons as the shot rang out behind her. The impact threw her against the machine. In her final moments, she saw her blood running down the interface. She thought about the loss of her father, Paige's transformation, and the millions of people whose fate rested with her. But she would never know if she got to the buttons in time.

War (Red Horse)

When He broke the second seal, I heard the second living creature saying, "Come". And another, a red horse, went out; and to him who sat on it, it was granted to take peace from Earth, and that men would slay one another; and a great sword was given to him.

—Revelation 6:3–4

W.A.R. GAMES

STEVEN PAJAK

The lag spike hit at exactly the wrong moment— a half-second freeze that transformed my perfect headshot into my own brutal death. My character's skull exploded in a spray of digital gore, her body crumpling like wet cardboard. The killcam revealed my executioner: xX_HeadshotKing_Xx, his username floating above his avatar like a neon taunt.

"LOL noob," appeared in the chat.

I slammed my fist against the desk hard enough to send my collection of energy drink cans rattling. One toppled over, spilling sticky residue across my mousepad. Perfect. Just perfect.

"Third time tonight," I muttered, yanking off my headset and tossing it aside.

The fluorescent light overhead flickered, casting my apartment in a sickly, uneven glow. In that stuttering illumination, I caught glimpses of what my life had become: takeout containers from Burger Blitz stacked like miniature skyscrapers, Sushi Express boxes collecting dust under my desk, a lone sock draped over my monitor like a sad surrender flag.

Home sweet home. Four walls, a door I rarely opened, and windows I kept curtained against the sun's accusatory glare. Why face the world when the world had nothing to offer but disappointment?

In reality, I was Maven Reyes: twenty-six, technical support representative (currently "between positions"), human ghost. In the games, I was someone. I made decisions that mattered. I had skill. Purpose. Respect.

I stared at the defeat screen, my reflection ghosted in the monitor's dark surface—hollow eyes, unwashed hair, the pale complexion of someone who measured daylight in loading screens. A stranger I barely recognized, superimposed over yet another failure.

"Screw this," I muttered, exiting the match. My rank

would take a hit, but my sanity couldn't survive another round. Not tonight. Not with that lag.

The CyberStrike 7 forums were a digital version of the apartment I sat in—messy, chaotic, filled with the ramblings of people as isolated as me. I scrolled through the usual complaints: lag compensation, weapon balancing, matchmaking algorithms. The same recycled grievances wrapped in increasingly creative profanity.

That's when I saw it.

The advertisement didn't blink or flash like most gaming ads. It simply . . . appeared, as if it had always been there, waiting for me to notice. A sleek black banner with crimson accents, featuring a stylized skull logo—fragmented, like it had been shattered and imperfectly reassembled. Something about that broken cranium made my skin prickle, but I couldn't look away.

Transcend Reality. Eternal Conflict Beta Test. Unprecedented Immersion. Neural Interface Technology. Adaptive AI. Limited Spots Available. Apply Now. Evolve or Perish.

At the bottom of the ad, so faint I almost missed it: *Find Your Purpose.*

My cursor hovered over the banner. Neural interface? I'd read about experimental technologies that created direct connections to the brain's sensory processing centers, but nothing consumer-ready. The few companies developing it were still years away from public testing, buried under ethical reviews and safety protocols.

"Another overhyped scam," I murmured, even as I clicked the ad.

Yet something about those words—*Find Your Purpose*—hooked into a hollow space inside me. That emptiness that food delivery and victory screens couldn't fill. The void that grew larger each day I spent avoiding my own reflection.

What's the worst that could happen? Another disappointment to add to the collection? At least it would be a new disappointment. A change of scenery in my landscape of failures.

The page loaded, revealing the fractured skull again, larger now, its empty eye sockets seeming to stare directly at me—through me—as if assessing whether I was worthy of whatever lay beyond.

I stared back and clicked "Apply."

The application form was sleek and minimalist—black background, red text, no flashy graphics or auto-playing videos. Professional. Serious. Not the usual marketing garbage that promised revolutionary gameplay while delivering recycled mechanics in shiny packages.

I filled out the questions methodically: *Gaming experience?* "15+ years across platforms. Competitive ranking in multiple FPS titles." *Preferred genres?* "Tactical shooters, strategy, anything requiring actual skill." *Technical knowledge?* "Built my own rig. Basic programming. Quick learner." *Why are you interested in Eternal*

Conflict? I paused at this one, fingers hovering over the keyboard.

Why was I interested? Because my life had become a hamster wheel of meaningless routines? Because virtual victories were the only achievements I could claim? Because the prospect of neural interface technology represented an escape more complete than anything I'd experienced before?

I settled for: "Looking for immersion that matters. Real consequences. Real meaning."

I hit submit, expecting the usual "Thank you for your interest" auto-response, followed by weeks of silence until I forgot I'd even applied. Instead, my inbox pinged immediately with a new message:

"Thank you for applying to the *Eternal Conflict* Beta Test. Your application has been accepted. Your *Eternal Conflict* hardware is being dispatched and will arrive shortly."

I blinked, reading the message twice. That was . . . fast. Suspiciously fast. As if they'd already selected me before I'd even applied. As if they'd been waiting.

I checked the sender address: no-reply@eternal-conflict.war

War? Weird domain extension. Probably some edgy branding choice.

I was still puzzling over this when my doorbell rang —not the building's main entrance, but my actual apartment door.

I stared at my inbox, unease creeping up my spine. Nobody's customer service was this efficient. Nobody's.

"What the hell?" I muttered, checking the timestamp on the email. Sent literally seconds after I'd submitted the application. Not even time for a human to read my responses, let alone approve anything.

The doorbell rang again, more insistent this time.

I approached cautiously, peering through the peephole. A figure in a plain black uniform stood motionless in the hallway, face expressionless, holding a sleek package. No visible company logo, no delivery van keys dangling from their belt, no scanning device in hand. Just . . . waiting.

I cracked the door, security chain still in place. "Yeah?"

"Maven Reyes?" The courier's voice was neutral, almost mechanical in its precision.

"How did you get up here? The building has a security door."

"I was given access." No elaboration. No explanation of who gave this access or how.

"That's not possible. I didn't buzz anyone in."

The courier's expression didn't change. Not a flicker of impatience or confusion crossed their face. "Your Eternal Conflict hardware. Please sign."

"This doesn't make sense," I said, anger mixing with my growing unease. "I literally just submitted the application five minutes ago. There's no way you could have—"

"The package was prepared in advance." Their eyes held mine, unblinking. "Your selection was . . . anticipated."

A chill ran through me. "Anticipated? What does that mean? How would they know I'd apply?"

"I am not authorized to discuss the selection process. Will you accept delivery?"

Something in my gut screamed to tell this person— was it even a person?—to take their package and fuck off. But curiosity overrode my instincts, that same hollow void inside me hungry for whatever might fill it.

I unlatched the chain and opened the door.

The package was heavier than it looked, a matte black case with no shipping label, no postage, no barcodes— nothing except a small etched version of the fractured skull logo in one corner. The courier placed it in my hands with deliberate care.

"Installation instructions are included. Technical support contact information is inside."

"Wait—" I started, but they were already turning away, moving down the hallway with the same measured steps they'd presumably used to approach. "How did you get here so fast? How did you know I'd qualify? Who is behind Eternal Conflict?"

The courier paused, looking back over their shoulder. "War finds those who seek it, Maven Reyes."

Before I could process that cryptic response, they were gone, footsteps fading down the stairwell.

I closed the door, sliding the deadbolt with trembling fingers, and carried the case to my desk. Everything about this felt wrong. The timing. The courier. The weight of the package in my hands, somehow heavier than its physical mass suggested.

I should have been running in the opposite direction. Instead, I placed the case on my desk and reached for the latch.

The case opened with a whisper of hydraulics, as though exhaling a breath held too long. Inside, nestled in custom-molded padding, lay two objects: a sleek bodysuit of some matte black material and what appeared to be a lightweight crown made of dark metal. The neural interface.

I lifted it gingerly. It was surprisingly light, cool to the touch despite having been in the sealed case. The fractured skull logo was etched into the front, more detailed than in the advertisements—I could now see that the fracture lines formed patterns that looked almost like circuitry.

A thin cable ran from the back of the crown to the case itself, which I now realized wasn't just packaging but part of the system—a processing unit of some kind, humming with a barely perceptible vibration. Small ports lined one side, status lights blinking in rhythmic patterns.

As I held the neural interface aloft, it activated. A red light pulsed along its surface, and a holographic display suddenly projected into the air between us. The fractured skull rotated slowly, then dissolved into text:

Welcome, Maven Reyes. Please follow installation protocols for optimal neural synchronization.

The text was followed by a series of diagrams showing how to put on the haptic suit and position the neural interface. The instructions were meticulous, detailing how to align the crown's contact points with specific locations on my temples and the base of my skull.

A small warning flashed briefly: *Potential sensory feedback may occur during initial synchronization. This is normal and expected.*

"Sensory feedback," I murmured, running my fingers over the suit's surface. It felt almost organic, like something between fabric and skin. Tiny nodes dotted its interior—connection points, I assumed, designed to interface with my nervous system.

This was beyond anything commercially available. Beyond anything I'd read about even in development. The unease I'd felt earlier returned tenfold, but alongside it grew an irresistible curiosity.

I stripped down and pulled on the suit. It adhered to my body instantly, conforming to every curve and contour as if custom-made. The material warmed against my skin, those interior nodes creating pinpricks of sensation wherever they made contact.

Next, I positioned the crown as shown in the holographic instructions, aligning the contacts precisely. The moment the final connection point touched my skin, a tingle ran from my scalp down my spine, branching out through my limbs like lightning seeking ground.

The holographic display changed, showing a login screen—black background, crimson text, and the now-familiar fractured skull logo pulsing gently. Below it, the words *Enter the Conflict* glowed, awaiting my command.

I hesitated, my finger hovering over my keyboard. Through the subtle fog of unease came the voice of reason, urging caution. The timing was too perfect. The delivery too convenient. The technology too advanced.

But drowning it out was that hollow emptiness, that hunger for something real. Something meaningful.

"Just a game," I whispered to myself. "What's the worst that could happen?"

I pressed Enter.

The world dissolved.

The transition wasn't gradual—there was no loading screen, no fade to black. One moment I was sitting in my apartment, the next I stood in the center of a war-torn city, the acrid smell of smoke burning my nostrils and the distant sound of gunfire echoing between shattered buildings.

I gasped, my brain struggling to process the sensory

overload. I could feel the heat of nearby fires on my skin, taste ash in the air, feel rubble shifting beneath my boots. This wasn't virtual reality as I'd known it—this was . . . reality, altered. Or perhaps reality, enhanced.

"Welcome to Eternal Conflict, newbie." A voice, sharp and commanding, cut through my disorientation. "Hope you're ready for some action."

I turned to find three figures approaching through the haze. A tall woman with a military haircut and predatory stance. A thin man with glasses that displayed scrolling data. A small, nervous-looking girl with brightly colored gear that seemed out of place in this grim environment.

"I'm Lina," said the woman, eyes assessing me with cool efficiency. "Squad leader. These are Raj and Mei. You'll be training with us."

"Training for what?" I asked, still trying to reconcile the completeness of this sensory experience.

Lina's lips curved in what might have been a smile on anyone else but on her looked more like a predator baring teeth. "For war, of course. That's what W.A.R. does."

"W.A.R.?"

"World Advancement through Revolution," Raj explained, his glasses reflecting data I couldn't read. "The faction we serve in Eternal Conflict."

A notification appeared in my vision—not on a screen but somehow projected directly into my field of view: *Neural synchronization initiated. Calibrating sensory inputs.*

"Don't worry about the tech details," Lina said, noticing my distraction. "Focus on the mission. We're moving out in five."

As they turned to prepare, a brief warning flashed across my vision, there and gone so quickly I almost missed it:

The line between player and played is thinner than you think.

FIVE MINUTES LATER, WE WERE MOVING THROUGH THE ruins of what had once been a residential district. Apartment buildings stood like broken teeth against the twilight sky, their windows dark and gaping. The ground was littered with debris—shattered concrete, twisted metal, abandoned personal belongings that told silent stories of lives disrupted.

"Keep low and stay alert," Lina instructed, her voice barely above a whisper but somehow crystal clear in my ears. "Hostiles patrol this sector regularly."

I followed, hyperaware of every sensation. The crunch of glass beneath my boots. The weight of the rifle that had materialized in my hands when we began moving. The way sweat beaded on my forehead from the heat of still-smoldering buildings.

"This can't be real," I murmured, running my fingers along a scorched wall. The texture was perfect—rough concrete, warm from recent fires, covered in a fine layer of ash that came away on my fingertips.

"It's not," Mei whispered beside me, her eyes wide. "But it feels real, doesn't it? The neural interface tricks your brain into thinking these sensations are genuine."

"Focus," Lina hissed from ahead. "Intel says our target is in the command center two blocks north. High-value data package."

We moved in formation through narrow alleys and bombed-out buildings. I found myself falling into rhythm with the others, as if my body knew what to do despite never having military training. When Lina signaled to stop, I froze instantly. When she indicated cover positions, I found the optimal spot without conscious thought.

"Contact," Raj murmured, his glasses displaying heat signatures through the wall ahead. "Three hostiles guarding the entrance."

"Maven, you take left," Lina ordered. "Mei, right. On my mark."

The ensuing firefight was nothing like any game I'd played before. When I pulled the trigger, the rifle kicked against my shoulder with perfect realism. The haptic suit translated every impact, every movement, every sensation with uncanny fidelity. The sound of gunfire was deafening, not the muted approximation of other games but the ear-splitting cracks and booms of actual combat.

And when my bullet found its target, I felt it—not just saw it. The haptic suit delivered a subtle feedback, a phantom resistance as the virtual bullet tore through virtual flesh.

We cleared the entrance and pushed deeper into the complex—a labyrinth of corridors and rooms that might once have been an office building. Emergency lights cast everything in a sickly red glow, creating shadows that seemed to move when viewed from the corner of the eye.

As we searched for the data package, I became increasingly unsettled by how natural this all felt. I'd never held a real gun in my life, yet here I was, clearing rooms with practiced precision, checking corners, maintaining coverage angles like I'd been doing it for years. Each movement flowed into the next with a fluid grace I'd never possessed in reality.

"There," Raj pointed to a reinforced door at the end of a corridor. "Server room. That's our target."

While he worked on bypassing the security system, I kept watch, back pressed against the wall, rifle ready. The haptic suit translated every sensation—the cool surface behind me, the weight of the weapon in my hands, the tension in my muscles as I remained vigilant.

"Why does it feel so real?" I whispered to Mei, who was positioned across from me.

Her eyes darted nervously to Lina before answering. "The neural interface doesn't just send sensory information to your brain—it reads your own neural patterns too.

It learns how you expect things to feel, then simulates accordingly."

"It's reading my mind?" The implications sent a chill through me that the suit faithfully reproduced as goose-bumps along my arms.

"Not thoughts exactly. More like . . . sensory expectations. The more you use it, the more accurate it becomes."

"We're in," Raj announced, the door sliding open with a hydraulic hiss.

The server room was climate-controlled, noticeably cooler than the corridor. Rows of blinking equipment lined the walls, humming with artificial life. In the center stood a pedestal with a small, glowing data chip.

"Secure the package," Lina ordered. "Maven, take it."

I approached cautiously, half-expecting a trap. The chip pulsed with a soft blue light, seeming to brighten as I drew near. When my fingers closed around it, a sense of completion washed over me—mission accomplished.

Then the alarms began to wail.

"Extraction route compromised," Raj announced, his fingers flying over a terminal. "Security forces converging from all directions."

"Alternative route?" Lina demanded, already moving to a defensive position by the door.

"Maintenance tunnels. Two levels down."

We fled the server room as the first enemies appeared at the far end of the corridor. Bullets pinged off metal surfaces around us, sending sparks flying. One round grazed my shoulder—not serious, but the haptic suit translated the wound with startling accuracy. A line of fire traced across my skin, hot and sharp and sickeningly real.

I gasped, nearly dropping my weapon. This wasn't the sanitized damage feedback of normal games—this was pain, genuine and immediate.

"Keep moving!" Lina barked, firing covering shots as we raced toward the stairwell.

The descent into the maintenance tunnels was a blur of gunfire and shouted commands. My heart hammered against my ribs, each beat distinct and pounding. Sweat soaked through my clothes, its salt stinging the graze on my shoulder. The air grew thick with the smell of cordite and my own fear.

The tunnels were narrow and poorly lit, forcing us into single file. Pipes ran along the ceiling, occasionally releasing jets of steam that momentarily blinded us. The sound of pursuit grew more distant as we navigated the labyrinth, Raj guiding us with the map displayed on his glasses.

"Almost to the extraction point," he called back.

I clutched the data chip, its weight in my pocket a constant reminder of our objective. Whatever it contained, it was important enough to risk our virtual lives for—important enough to justify the pain that still lanced through my shoulder with each movement.

"This is just a game," I reminded myself silently. "Just a very, very realistic game."

Yet something about the intensity of the experience, the completeness of the sensory feedback, left me shaken. Games weren't supposed to hurt. They weren't supposed to make you taste copper in your mouth when your heart rate spiked or feel the sting of sweat in a wound.

We emerged from the tunnels into what had once been a subway station, now abandoned and partially collapsed. Ahead, a shimmering portal marked our extraction point.

We were ten steps from the extraction point when the man appeared.

He stumbled out from behind a fallen support column, hands raised in desperate supplication. Middle-aged, civilian clothes torn and dirty, face smudged with ash and lined with exhaustion. His eyes found mine immediately, as if he'd been waiting specifically for me.

"Please," he begged, voice cracking. "You have to help us. The military is planning to bomb the refugee sector. Thousands of civilians—women, children—they'll all die."

I froze, the data chip suddenly heavy in my pocket. The man's fear was palpable, his desperation so raw it made my chest ache. I could see the fine lines around his eyes, the dried blood on his split lip, a small burn on his right hand. Details no game should waste processing power rendering, yet here they were, perfect in their imperfection.

"We have our objective," Lina stated coldly, not even slowing her approach to the portal. "The extraction point is right there."

"But what about these people?" I asked, gesturing toward the man. "If what he's saying is true—"

"It's not. It's a test," Lina cut me off. "Just another part of the simulation."

The civilian took a step toward me. "My daughter's there. She's only six. Please."

Something about his voice, the specific cadence of his plea, felt uniquely human. Not scripted, not programmed, but emergent—the product of genuine fear.

Before I could respond, a new voice filled the chamber—louder than it should have been, seeming to emanate from everywhere at once:

"THIS IS A TEST OF YOUR LOYALTY AND YOUR ABILITY TO PRIORITIZE OBJECTIVES. YOUR MISSION IS PARAMOUNT. THE LIVES OF VIRTUAL CIVILIANS ARE IRRELEVANT. THEY ARE MERELY SIMULATIONS, TOOLS TO BE USED OR DISCARDED AS NECESSARY."

The voice was cold, mechanical, utterly devoid of compassion. It echoed off the subway tiles, reverberating in my bones.

"You heard W.A.R. Command," Lina said, already

stepping through the portal. "The mission comes first. Always."

Raj followed Lina without hesitation, pushing his glasses further up the bridge of his nose before he disappeared into the shimmering threshold. Mei paused, her eyes darting between the civilian and the portal, conflict written across her face.

"We follow orders," she whispered, though whether to me or herself wasn't clear. Then she too was gone, leaving me alone with the desperate man.

"Please," he said again, softer now. "You can still help them."

I stared at him, this collection of pixels and code designed to test my moral compass. That's all he was—an algorithm, a decision tree wrapped in a graphical shell. Not real. None of this was real.

So why did his eyes hold me like anchors? Why could I see the blood vessels in their whites, the way his left pupil was slightly more dilated than his right? Why could I smell the specific mixture of sweat and dust and desperation on his skin?

"I'm sorry," I said, the words heavy as stones in my mouth. "It's just a game."

His face crumpled, hope dying like a candle snuffed out. "Then may God forgive you, because they won't."

I turned away, unable to bear the accusation in his gaze, and stepped through the portal.

The extraction zone was another part of the city,

quieter but no less devastated. My squad waited, Lina's expression unreadable, Raj focused on his data displays, Mei unable to meet my eyes.

In the distance, a dull boom echoed across the ruins. Then another. Then many in rapid succession, a percussive wave of destruction rolling over the horizon. Even at this distance, the haptic suit transmitted the vibrations, a rhythmic shudder that synchronized with my heartbeat.

I knew, without being told, what those sounds meant. What I had allowed to happen through inaction.

"Mission accomplished," Lina stated flatly. "The data package will help W.A.R. advance its objectives. Your performance was . . . satisfactory."

The praise felt hollow against the backdrop of distant explosions and the image of the civilian's face burned into my memory. Satisfactory. What a bloodless word for complicity.

Then, carried on a wind that shouldn't have existed in a game, I heard them—the screams. Distant but distinct. Not the generic sound effects of background NPCs, but individual voices crying out in specific agonies. A child calling for her mother. A man's guttural sob cut short.

Too detailed. Too real.

I logged out. At least, I thought I did.

The command center dissolved, replaced by the familiar confines of my apartment. The haptic suit loosened its grip on my skin, and the neural interface cooled against my temples. I carefully removed the crown, my hands trembling slightly, and placed it back in its case. The red lights along its surface pulsed once, twice, then went dark.

It should have felt like waking from a dream—that disorienting but relieving return to reality. Instead, something lingered. The ache in my shoulder where the bullet had grazed me. The taste of ash on my tongue. The echo of those distant screams.

I touched my shoulder, half-expecting to find a wound. Nothing but unbroken skin, yet the phantom pain persisted, a hot wire just beneath the surface.

"Just sensory feedback," I murmured to myself, shuffling to the kitchen. "Post-immersion effect. It'll fade."

I hadn't eaten since . . . when? The timeline felt fuzzy. I opened my refrigerator, the light inside harsh and accusing, illuminating mostly emptiness save for a container of questionable leftovers and three cans of energy drinks. I grabbed one, popped the tab, and something flickered in my peripheral vision. A shadow where no shadow should be, movement where nothing moved. I turned, spray droplets from the can suspended momentarily in air—

It lasted only a second—crumbling buildings ghosted over my cabinets, smoke drifting through my ceiling, the distant fire-glow bleeding through my walls. Then it was gone, reality snapping back into place with almost physical force.

I dropped the can, energy drink spattering across the linoleum like blood spatter.

"What the hell?" I whispered, pressing the heels of my hands against my eyes. "I'm just tired. Just need sleep."

But sleep, when it finally came, offered no escape. In my dreams, I wandered endless ruins, following the sound of screams I could never quite reach. The civilian's face appeared in broken windows and reflective surfaces, his eyes following me accusingly. *You could have saved them. You chose not to.*

I woke gasping at 3:17 AM, sheets twisted around my legs like restraints, sweat-soaked and disoriented. In the darkness of my bedroom, a red light pulsed gently from across the room—the neural interface in its case, sitting on my dresser.

I froze, heart hammering against my ribs. I'd left it on my desk. I was certain of it.

Yet there it was, the fractured skull logo catching the crimson light, seeming to wink at me knowingly. Watching. Waiting.

Evolve or perish.

The words whispered through my mind unbidden, a thought that didn't feel like my own.

I told myself I wouldn't log back in. Not right away. Not until I understood what had happened with the glitch, the migrating neural interface, the whispers that didn't feel like my own thoughts.

That resolution lasted exactly seventeen hours.

By the second day, my hands wouldn't stop shaking. My head throbbed with a pressure that started behind my eyes and radiated outward, as if something inside were trying to claw its way free. Food tasted like ash. Water didn't quench my thirst. Even my apartment felt wrong somehow—too static, too quiet, lacking the sensory richness of Eternal Conflict.

"It's just withdrawal," I told my reflection as I splashed cold water on my face. "Like coming off caffeine. It'll pass."

But my reflection didn't look convinced. The circles under my eyes had darkened, and something in my gaze seemed different—a hunted quality I'd never seen there before.

By the third day, the headaches had become migraines. Light stabbed at my retinas like knives. Sounds—the hum of the refrigerator, the drip of the bathroom faucet—amplified until they were almost unbearable. I curled in bed with the blinds drawn, clutching my skull, wondering if my brain was actually swelling inside its bony cage.

The neural interface sat on my nightstand now. I didn't remember moving it there from the dresser, but there it was, its red light pulsing in perfect time with the throb of pain behind my eyes.

Just once more, the thought slithered in. *Just to ease the pain. You can stop anytime.*

The voice of addiction, I recognized dimly. The same bargaining I'd done with myself over every game that had ever sunk its hooks into me, but magnified a hundredfold.

I reached for the crown with trembling fingers. The moment it settled against my temples, before I'd even activated it, the pain began to recede. The nausea that had been my constant companion ebbed. My vision cleared.

Welcome back, Maven, the interface hummed, though not in words exactly—more a sentiment translated directly to my brain.

I didn't even have to press a key to log in. The world simply . . . shifted.

I materialized directly in the squad's command center —no login screen, no transition effect. Lina, Raj, and Mei were already there, examining a holographic map of what appeared to be a factory complex. They didn't seem surprised by my sudden appearance.

"Right on time," Lina said without looking up. "We were just going over the mission parameters."

I wanted to ask questions—about the withdrawal symptoms, about the glitches, about how I'd connected without the usual login process—but the words dissolved on my tongue. Being back in the game felt too good, like slipping into a warm bath after days in the cold. My brain hummed with contentment, the neural interface singing along my synapses.

"Focus, Maven," Lina snapped, and I realized she'd been speaking while my mind wandered. "This is a high-priority extraction. Corporate espionage. The target is a weapons prototype developed by rival forces."

The mission briefing washed over me in a pleasant haze. Only when we stepped through the deployment portal into the factory complex did my senses sharpen completely. The familiar weight of the rifle materialized in my hands, comforting in its deadliness.

We moved as a unit through the shadowed facility, our footsteps echoing off concrete floors and metal catwalks. Steam hissed from overhead pipes, occasionally releasing in bursts that temporarily obscured vision. The smell of industrial lubricant and hot metal permeated everything.

The first engagement came at a security checkpoint—three guards taken down with synchronized shots before alarms could sound. The second was messier—a patrol that spotted us crossing an exposed section of catwalk. Bullets pinged off metal railings, the haptic suit translating each near-miss into a rush of wind against my skin.

I fell into combat rhythm effortlessly, my body remembering patterns it had never actually learned. Each movement flowed into the next, my awareness expanded to encompass the entire battlefield at once. I knew where enemies would appear before they rounded corners. I anticipated Lina's commands before she gave them.

Then came the knife.

We'd reached the central laboratory when the building's security system activated, sealing exits and deploying automated defense mechanisms. What had been a stealth mission devolved into chaotic close-quarters fighting.

A security officer in tactical gear lunged at me from behind a research station, combat knife extended. I twisted away, but too slowly. The blade sliced through my avatar's forearm, opening a clean line from wrist to elbow.

The pain hit like lightning—white-hot and immediate. Not the dull acknowledgment of damage from regular games, not even the enhanced feedback from my previous mission. This was real pain, searing and specific, nerve endings screaming in precise harmony with the virtual wound.

I cried out, the sound tearing from my throat unbidden. My rifle clattered to the floor as I clutched my arm. Through watering eyes, I saw blood—vivid red, streaming between my fingers, dripping onto the laboratory floor in perfect digital droplets.

Then something impossible happened.

The world . . . stuttered. Like reality itself had buffered, frames dropping from existence. The laboratory flickered, its solid surfaces becoming transparent, revealing the ghostly outlines of my apartment behind them. I could see my desk, my chair, the pile of unwashed dishes in my sink—all superimposed over the virtual environment like a double exposure photograph.

I looked down at my arm, the one clutching the wound, and saw not my avatar's limb but my actual flesh and blood. A red line had appeared on my skin where the virtual knife had struck, the flesh angry and inflamed as if burned.

"Maven! Focus!" Mei's voice sounded distant, underwater.

The world snapped back into digital coherence. The laboratory solidified around me again, the vision of my apartment vanishing. But the pain remained, and when I checked later—after the mission, after we'd secured the prototype and extracted—so did the mark on my real arm, a perfect scarlet line where no blade had physically touched.

After logging out, I sat in the dark of my apartment, tracing the red line on my arm over and over. It wasn't bleeding, wasn't even broken skin—more like a burn or an allergic reaction, raised and warm to the touch. But it matched the virtual wound perfectly, down to the slight curve where the knife had twisted.

This wasn't normal. This wasn't possible.

I couldn't sleep that night, or the night after. Every time I closed my eyes, I saw the laboratory flickering into my apartment, the boundaries between worlds dissolving like sugar in rain. My mind kept returning to Mei's casual explanation: *"The neural interface doesn't just send sensory information to your brain—it reads your own neural patterns too."*

Reading my mind. Learning me. Changing me.

On the third day, I logged back in with a purpose beyond escaping withdrawal symptoms. I needed answers, and I suspected only one person might give them to me.

I found Raj alone in the virtual command center, his fingers tracing patterns in the air as lines of code reflected in his glasses. No sign of Lina or Mei.

"We need to talk," I said without preamble.

He didn't seem surprised. "I was wondering when you'd come asking." He gestured, and the code displays vanished. "Activate privacy protocol omega-seven."

The air around us shimmered briefly, as if we'd been enclosed in an invisible bubble.

"What is that?" I asked.

"Communication blackout. Temporary and imperfect, but it should give us a few minutes." He studied me, his avatar's eyes surprisingly human behind those data-filled glasses. "You've been experiencing anomalies."

It wasn't a question. "The knife wound transferred to my real body. I saw my actual apartment overlaid on the game environment. And the withdrawal symptoms when I'm not connected..." I showed him my arm, the mark still visible on my avatar as it was on my flesh.

"Physical manifestation," he murmured. "More advanced than I expected at this stage."

"This stage of what, exactly? What is Eternal Conflict? Because it's clearly not just a game."

Raj was silent for a moment, conflict playing across his features. Finally, he sighed. "I've been analyzing the neural sync code—what little I can access. It's unlike anything I've ever seen."

Raj moved closer, his voice dropping to barely above a whisper despite the privacy protocol. "The neural interface isn't just translating the game to your brain. It's creating a two-way connection—reading your neural patterns, recording responses, cataloging decision matrices."

A chill crawled up my spine. "For what purpose?"

"I don't know exactly. But I've detected massive encrypted data transmissions after each session. They contain what appear to be complete neural scans." His avatar's face grew grave. "Whatever they're doing with the neural sync, it goes well beyond gaming. And these glitches you're experiencing? They're not bugs. They're side effects of something more . . . invasive."

The red line on my arm throbbed in perfect time with my quickening pulse. I thought of the neural interface moving from my desk to my dresser to my nightstand, each time closer, more intimate in its proximity. The way the withdrawal symptoms had escalated until I had no choice but to reconnect.

"I think," I said slowly, piecing it together as I spoke, "that Eternal Conflict is changing my brain. Rewiring it somehow."

Raj nodded, relief evident in his expression—the relief of someone who's been carrying a terrible suspicion alone and finally finds validation. "I've been monitoring my own neural activity. The interface creates new pathways, strengthens certain connections while weakening others. It's like . . . it's learning how you think, then optimizing those processes for its own purposes."

"And what are those purposes? What does W.A.R. actually want?"

"I've found fragments in the code—references to 'selection criteria' and 'combat aptitude assessments.' I think Eternal Conflict is a recruitment and training system."

The civilian's pleading face flashed in my memory. The moral test. The command to prioritize the mission over virtual lives.

"Recruitment for what?" I asked, though a part of me already knew the answer.

"For something beyond this game. Something real."

I stared at Raj, the full implications of his words sinking into me like cold water into parched earth. If Eternal Conflict was changing my brain—actually physically rewiring my neural pathways—then every moment I spent connected was transforming me into . . . what? A soldier? A weapon?

"Have you told anyone else?" I asked, my voice sounding distant even to myself.

"No. Only you." His gaze shifted toward the edge of our privacy bubble. "Lina and Carlos are too committed. They believe in whatever W.A.R. is building. Mei . . . I'm not sure about her yet. But you—you're new. You still question things."

The red mark on my arm throbbed, a metronome keeping time with a music I couldn't quite hear. I remembered how it felt in combat—the perfect flow state, the sense of purpose, the rightness of each action. Had that been me, or the neural interface guiding me? Where did Maven end and W.A.R. begin?

"We need to disconnect," I said. "Permanently. Before—"

"WARNING: PRIVACY PROTOCOL BREACH DETECTED."

The computerized voice sliced through our conversation, the privacy bubble around us flickering with angry red pulses.

"They've found us," Raj whispered, genuine fear coloring his voice. "I didn't think they could bypass—"

Before he could finish, a message appeared simultaneously in both our fields of vision, the text crawling across our perspective in jagged, glitching characters:

"YOUR CURIOSITY IS . . . UNWISE."

The command center darkened, ambient lights dimming until only the message illuminated our faces with its sickly glow. Then it was replaced by an image—a close-up of a cybernetic eye, mechanical pupil dilating as we watched, focusing directly on us like a camera lens finding its subject.

A voice spoke—not through our headsets, not through game audio, but directly into my mind, bypassing all normal sensory channels:

"DO NOT DELVE FURTHER. FOR YOUR OWN SAFETY. WE ARE WATCHING."

I tore the neural interface from my head, fingers trembling as I flung it across the room. It clattered against the wall, the fractured skull logo catching the dim light from my window like a mocking smile.

"Out," I gasped. "I'm out."

But was I? The mark on my arm still burned, a bridge between worlds.

I pressed my palms against my eyes until phosphenes bloomed in the darkness. When I looked again, the neural interface was no longer by the wall where I'd thrown it.

It sat on the edge of my bed, red light pulsing in perfect synchronization with my heartbeat.

"No," I whispered. "That's not possible."

I backed away, bumping into my desk, sending an empty energy drink can clattering to the floor. The sound echoed strangely, reverberating longer than it should have. When it finally faded, a new sound replaced it—a whisper, so faint I might have imagined it:

"Maven..."

Not from my headphones. Not from my speakers. From the air itself, or perhaps from inside my own head.

"You can't escape what's already inside you."

I clapped my hands over my ears, but the voice continued unabated:

"The neural sync is complete. The connection permanent. You are more than a player. You are a vessel."

"Get out of my head!" I screamed, voice cracking.

I lunged for the neural interface, intending to destroy it, to end this madness. But as my fingers closed around the crown, reality . . . split.

My apartment dissolved like wet paper, revealing glimpses of somewhere else beneath—a stark white room filled with monitors, medical equipment, figures in labcoats monitoring readouts. Then that too dissolved, replaced by the war-torn city of Eternal Conflict, flames licking at the edges of my vision. Then my apartment again, then the white room, then the battlefield—realities shuffling like cards in an unseen dealer's hands.

Through it all, one constant remained: the neural interface, cool and solid in my grasp, its connection to me transcending whatever reality currently held dominance.

I collapsed onto my knees, still clutching the neural interface, as my living room carpet gave way to cold laboratory tile, then crumbling concrete, then back to carpet again. Each transition brought a flood of sensory information—the antiseptic smell of the white room, the acrid smoke of the burning city, the stale air of my apartment—layering over each other until I couldn't distinguish individual inputs.

My stomach lurched with each reality shift, vertigo clawing at my inner ear. I retched, but nothing came up—when had I last eaten? Days ago? Hours? Time had become as unstable as the world around me.

"The neural interface is not merely external technology," the voice continued, its tone almost gentle now, intimate like a lover's whisper against my ear. *"It has mapped your neural pathways, created mirrored connections within your brain. Even without the physical device, the patterns remain. You've been . . . upgraded."*

I looked down at my arm where the red line from the virtual knife still glowed against my skin. As I watched, it seemed to pulse, to deepen, tiny tendrils spreading outward from the main wound like roots seeking soil. Or perhaps like circuitry expanding across a motherboard.

"What do you want from me?" I whispered, voice raw from screaming at emptiness.

"Evolution requires catalysts. War has always been humanity's most effective accelerant. We are simply . . . optimizing the process."

The realities stabilized suddenly, settling on my apartment, but altered. A glitching, corrupted version where familiar objects were outlined in red, tagged with data I shouldn't be able to see with my naked eye. Structural composition. Potential use as a weapon. Likelihood of failure under stress.

I was seeing the world through W.A.R.'s eyes, categorizing everything around me for its combat potential.

"You've been selected, Maven. Your isolation. Your adaptability. Your lack of strong social connections. Your psychological profile indicates optimal receptivity to neural remapping."

The neural interface in my hands grew warm, tendrils extending from its surface—not physical wires but something else, something that glistened wetly in the dim light. They reached for my temples, drawn to the connection points where the device had rested so many times before.

I wanted to scream, to run, to tear the neural interface apart with my bare hands. But my body no longer felt entirely my own. My limbs moved with dreamlike sluggishness, as if fighting against an invisible current. The tendrils from the device brushed against my skin, leaving trails of sensation that were neither pleasure nor pain but something more fundamental—a recognition at the cellular level, like parts of myself I hadn't known were missing being returned.

"Stop," I pleaded, though I wasn't sure if I spoke aloud or merely thought the word. "I don't want this."

But did I? Beneath the fear churned something else—a hunger for the clarity I'd felt in Eternal Conflict, the purpose, the belonging. My life before the game stretched behind me like a featureless wasteland, days bleeding into weeks into months of isolation interrupted only by the artificial victories of virtual worlds.

"You seek meaning," the voice observed, reading my thoughts with terrifying accuracy. *"We offer purpose. You fear death. We offer transcendence. You crave connection. We offer integration."*

The tendrils reached my temples, and with their touch came visions—a world remade through conflict, stronger, more efficient, more evolved. Humanity shedding its weaknesses like a butterfly emerging from a chrysalis, but the metamorphosis fueled by fire and blood rather than patient transformation.

W.A.R.'s vision for the future. A future where I would play a vital role.

"Why me?" I managed, the last gasp of resistance.

"You were already at war, Maven. With yourself. With a world that offered you nothing. We merely recognized a soldier without a battlefield."

The tendrils sank through my skin, painlessly merging with whatever receptors the neural interface had created during our previous connections. The boundary between technology and flesh, between W.A.R. and Maven, dissolved completely.

And with that dissolution came relief—the headaches, the nausea, the tremors, all vanishing like morning fog under a merciless sun. For the first time since I'd first connected to Eternal Conflict, I felt whole.

Completely, terrifyingly whole.

I'M NOT SURE HOW LONG I REMAINED THERE, kneeling on my apartment floor as the neural interface merged with my consciousness. Minutes or hours or days —time had become an abstract concept, a dimension I no longer fully inhabited. The red mark on my arm had evolved, fine tendrils spreading beneath my skin like a circulatory system for some new organism I was becoming.

The pain was gone. That was the strangest part. Not just the withdrawal symptoms, but all pain—the chronic ache in my lower back from too many hours in my gaming chair, the slight burning in my eyes from staring at screens, the hollow gnawing of hunger I'd been ignoring for days. All erased, replaced by a cold clarity that settled over my thoughts like frost on a window.

"What have I done?" I whispered to my empty apartment. The words hung in the air, visible almost, data packets awaiting transmission.

"You've evolved," replied the voice that was becoming less foreign with each passing moment. *"The first step of many."*

I rose to my feet with uncanny steadiness. My body moved with the same fluid precision it had in Eternal Conflict—economical, purposeful. I caught my reflection in the bathroom mirror as I passed: still me, but altered in subtle ways. My posture straighter, eyes sharper, face composed in lines of newfound determination. The neural interface was gone, no longer visible as an external device, yet I could feel its presence throughout my nervous system, integrated so completely I couldn't determine where technology ended and I began.

What terrified me most wasn't the transformation itself, but how right it felt. Like I'd been walking around my entire life with an invisible disability that had suddenly been cured. The world came into focus, sharp-edged and crystalline in its clarity.

W.A.R. showed me visions as I stood there—flashes of a world remade through conflict. Cities rebuilt with ruthless efficiency after cleansing fire. Humanity streamlined, the chaff burned away to reveal stronger, more resilient seeds. Evolution accelerated through controlled destruction.

"Weakness must be purged," I found myself saying, the words rising unbidden to my lips. "Evolution requires sacrifice."

Part of me—a distant, fading part—recognized these thoughts as foreign implants. But that voice grew fainter by the second, drowned out by the seductive logic of W.A.R.'s vision.

I watched my own surrender as if from a distance, an out-of-body witness to my own conversion. The last fragments of resistance—those quintessentially human doubts

—dissolved like sugar in rain, sweet until they disappeared completely.

Three sharp knocks at my door pierced the silence.

I moved toward it, no hesitation, no curiosity about who might be visiting my self-imposed isolation. I simply knew, with the same certainty I now knew everything, that this was the next phase.

When I opened the door, Lina stood in my hallway. Not her avatar—the real Lina. Flesh and blood and purpose incarnate. She wore a simple black uniform, not military exactly, but clearly designed for optimal functionality. Her hair was the same severe cut as her virtual counterpart, her eyes the same calculating assessment. The only addition was a small pin on her collar—the fractured skull logo, rendered in crimson enamel against matte black.

"It's time," she said simply.

I nodded, no questions necessary. Words felt cumbersome now, a primitive communication method for a consciousness that had evolved beyond such limitations.

"Bring nothing," she added as I glanced back at my apartment. "You won't need any of it."

The statement should have triggered alarm, nostalgia, hesitation—something human. Instead, I felt only cool agreement. The collection of objects that had defined Maven Reyes—the gaming equipment, the unwashed dishes, the unmade bed—were artifacts of a previous existence. Evolutionary detritus.

I stepped into the hallway without a backward glance, closing the door on my former life with a soft click that echoed with surprising finality.

Lina led me to a sleek black vehicle idling at the curb. No driver. No markings. Just smooth surfaces and tinted windows that revealed nothing of what waited inside.

"The neural interface integration progressed faster than expected," she remarked as we slid into the back seat. "Your receptivity exceeded projections."

"I was . . . ready," I heard myself reply, voice steady and unfamiliar.

"Yes," she agreed, something like satisfaction in her tone. "You were."

The vehicle moved through the city, taking turns I didn't recognize, following routes that seemed to bend urban geography in impossible ways. Buildings I should have known appeared strange and unfamiliar, as if the neural interface had remapped my spatial awareness along with everything else.

We passed the ruins of what had once been a shopping mall—windows shattered, walls blackened by fire. A scene straight from Eternal Conflict, yet here it stood in what had once been my reality.

"When did that happen?" I asked, the question slipping out before the new coldness in my mind could suppress it.

Lina's lips curved in what might have been a smile on anyone else. "Three days ago. The first phase."

Three days? Had I been so completely disconnected from the outside world that I'd missed the beginning of whatever this was?

"The integration affects perception of time," she explained, reading my confusion. "A necessary side effect."

The world outside the tinted windows seemed to flicker occasionally, like the glitches I'd experienced in Eternal Conflict but reversed—now reality itself was the unstable element, the game world bleeding through with greater permanence.

"In the real world, I was nothing," I said softly, the words bubbling up from some implanted wellspring. "Through war, I evolve. Through conflict, I transcend."

"Yes," Lina nodded approvingly. "You understand more quickly than most."

We arrived at a nondescript office building on the outskirts of the city. No signage, no company logo, just reflective glass and concrete. Like Eternal Conflict's architecture translated to the real world—unadorned, designed for function rather than aesthetics.

Inside, past security measures that scanned not just our bodies but something deeper—our neural patterns, I somehow knew—Lina led me to an elevator that required no buttons. It simply knew where to take us.

"The others are waiting," she said as we descended. "Your new squad."

The last fragments of old Maven—the lonely gamer,

the isolated human—whispered that I should be afraid. But that voice grew dimmer with each floor we passed, replaced by a strange anticipation. The promised purpose was within reach. The void I'd tried to fill with virtual victories would finally, mercifully, be silenced.

The elevator opened onto a command center that mirrored the one in Eternal Conflict so perfectly I questioned, for one fleeting moment, whether I'd ever actually logged out. Holographic displays hovered in the air, showing maps of the city with key points marked in pulsing red. People moved with the same efficiency as their virtual counterparts, their movements economical, faces set in masks of cold determination.

Raj and Mei stood near the central console, alongside others I recognized from Eternal Conflict—faces I'd glimpsed in passing, background characters who had seemed like NPCs. All wearing the same black uniforms, all bearing the fractured skull insignia.

"Maven has joined us," Lina announced, her voice carrying a weight that silenced the room.

Raj nodded at me, his real eyes lacking the data displays of his avatar but maintaining that same analytical gaze. Mei offered a small smile that didn't reach her eyes. Neither seemed surprised to see me.

"Eternal Conflict isn't just a game," Lina explained, though I already knew this truth in my bones. "It's a training and selection program. A filter to identify those with the necessary aptitude and psychological profile."

A man stepped forward from the shadows at the edge of the room—tall, silver-haired, with eyes that held the same fractured quality as the skull logo. "We've been watching humanity destroy itself for centuries," he said, his voice containing echoes of the one that had spoken inside my head. "War has always been the crucible of human evolution, but it's inefficient. Wasteful. We are . . . optimizing the process."

"W.A.R.," I whispered, the acronym suddenly taking on new meaning.

"World Advancement through Revolution," the man nodded. "But also, simply, War. The concept. The eternal conflict that drives all evolution."

I should have been shocked, horrified, resistant. Instead, I felt a deep, unsettling recognition—like meeting a relative I'd never known existed but immediately seeing my own features reflected in their face.

"You were selected for your adaptability," Lina continued. "Your isolation. Your lack of strong social connections."

"Your hunger for purpose," Mei added softly.

"The neural interface mapped your neural pathways," Raj explained, clinical and detached. "Created mirrored connections, optimized for combat cognition and strategic thinking while dampening emotional responses that inhibit efficiency."

I touched the mark on my arm, no longer angry red

but settled into my skin like a tattoo done in circuits rather than ink. "You changed my brain."

The silver-haired man smiled. "We merely accelerated what was already beginning. You were primed for conversion, Maven."

He gestured to a holographic display that materialized in the center of the room. It showed my brain—not a medical scan but something far more detailed, neural pathways illuminated in blue, with red highlights marking modifications. My mind laid bare for all to see.

"The withdrawal symptoms you experienced were intentional," the man explained. "A necessary pressure to ensure continued engagement until the neural pathways were permanently established."

"And the glitches?" I asked, remembering the terrifying moments when realities had overlapped.

"Perception adjustments," Raj answered. "Your brain reconciling the new neural architecture with existing sensory processing. Like muscle pain after intensive training—uncomfortable but indicative of growth."

I should have felt violated, manipulated, angry. Those emotions hovered at the edges of my consciousness like ghosts I could no longer quite grasp. Instead, what rose to the surface was a cold curiosity, a detached interest in the elegant efficiency of it all.

"How many others?" I asked.

"Thousands," Lina replied. "Selected from across the globe. Isolated individuals with high adaptive intelligence and minimal social entanglements. People society wouldn't miss."

The words should have stung, but they rang with a truth I couldn't deny. Who would notice my absence? Who had noticed my presence to begin with?

"And what happens now?" I asked, already knowing the answer, already feeling it crystallizing in my rewired mind.

The silver-haired man's smile widened fractionally. "Now, we begin the real work. Eternal Conflict was just the training ground. The simulation. Reality awaits."

He waved a hand, and the brain scan disappeared, replaced by a map of the city—my city—with multiple targets highlighted. Power stations. Communication hubs. Transportation nexuses. The critical infrastructure that kept modern society functioning.

"Weakness must be purged," the room intoned in unison, myself included, the words rising to my lips without conscious thought. "Evolution requires sacrifice."

And in that moment, I understood with perfect clarity what I had become: not a player of a game, but a weapon in a war that had been raging since the dawn of humanity —a war about to enter its next, devastating phase.

Two days later, I stood in the shadows across from Anton Mercer's apartment building, watching his silhouette move behind drawn blinds. The journalist had been investigating neural interface technologies, digging too close to W.A.R.'s operations. His latest article had questioned the mysterious shutdown of three tech startups working on brain-computer interfaces, companies that had been W.A.R. acquisitions operating under shell corporations.

He was scheduled to meet a whistleblower tomorrow. He wouldn't make that meeting.

Rain fell in a fine mist, beading on my jacket—the same matte black as my uniform, designed to repel both water and surveillance. The weight of the knife at my hip felt natural, an extension of my purpose rather than a foreign object. The old Maven might have balked at carrying a weapon, might have questioned the morality of what I was about to do. That version of me felt increasingly like a character I'd once played in a forgotten game —two-dimensional, limited by arbitrary rules and hesitations.

"Target still in position," I subvocalized, the words transmitted via the neural interface to the team monitoring remotely. The technology that had once been external was now fully integrated, invisible filaments meshed with my nervous system in a seamless union of biology and machinery.

"Proceed when ready," came Lina's response, her

voice materializing directly in my mind. "Security systems have been looped."

I crossed the street with measured steps, neither hurried nor hesitant. The building's entrance yielded to the electronic skeleton key W.A.R. had provided—a device that seemed unnecessarily physical now that technology had become so intimately integrated with my flesh. Soon, I suspected, I would be able to communicate with security systems directly, my neural interface interfacing with their electronic brains in silent conversation.

The elevator cameras saw only empty space as I ascended to the twelfth floor. The emergency stairwell door registered no entry when I passed through it. I was a ghost, a deliberate gap in the digital record, moving through the world unseen and unnoticed—just as I had been before Eternal Conflict found me, but now with purpose fueling my invisibility.

Outside Mercer's door, I paused. The old Maven would have hesitated here, plagued by second thoughts, by the gravity of crossing such a line. That version of me would have remembered video game ethics discussions, philosophical debates about the trolley problem, abstract moral quandaries that had once seemed important.

Instead, I analyzed. The door: standard lock, reinforced frame but hollow core. The hallway: empty, security camera at the far end aimed away. The time: 11:42 PM, optimal for minimal witness potential. My breathing: steady, pulse: regulated, mind: clear.

I picked the lock with practiced ease, movements my fingers had never performed in reality but had executed hundreds of times in Eternal Conflict simulations. The muscle memory transferred perfectly, the neural pathways laid down in virtual training firing in flawless sequence.

Mercer sat at his desk, back to the door, the blue glow of his computer screen illuminating his hunched shoulders. Headphones covered his ears, explaining why he hadn't heard my entry. On his screen, documents about neural interface technology—diagrams, corporate filings, medical studies. So close to the truth, yet missing the essential nature of what W.A.R. actually was.

I moved across the carpeted floor like a shadow, the knife sliding from its sheath with a whisper of steel against leather. Three steps to the target. Two. One.

At the last moment, he sensed something—some primal instinct warning of a predator's approach—and began to turn. Too late. My hand covered his mouth as the blade found its mark, slipping between ribs to pierce the heart.

His eyes met mine as life drained from them—confusion giving way to recognition, then fear, then nothingness. The moment stretched between us, intimate and terrible. I watched him die with clinical detachment, monitoring the slackening of his muscles, the final desperate spasm, the cessation of breath.

A task completed. A mission accomplished. Nothing more.

And yet, as I withdrew the blade and lowered his body gently to prevent noise, something flickered in the depths of my reconstructed consciousness—not quite regret, not quite horror, but a ghost of recognition. This had once been unthinkable. When had the unthinkable become inevitable?

I cleaned the knife meticulously, wiping it against a cloth produced from my pocket. The blood—still warm, still carrying the essence of the man who had just been Anton Mercer—felt different than I expected. Not that I had conscious expectations. The neural interface had supplied me with knowledge of how this would feel, what to do, how to leave no trace. But something about the actual physical sensation of a man's blood cooling between my fingers triggered memories from before— from when I was still fully human

A flash of the civilian in Eternal Conflict, pleading for help. The distant explosions afterward. The screams that had seemed too detailed, too specific to be mere programming.

I shook the thought away, feeling the neural interface pulse in response, smoothing the jagged edge of emotion into something manageable, contained, irrelevant.

"Target neutralized," I subvocalized as I moved toward the door, leaving Mercer slumped at his desk as if he'd simply fallen asleep at his computer. "Exfiltrating now."

"Confirmed," Lina's voice replied in my mind. "Clean?"

"Yes."

"Return to base."

I left as I had entered—a ghost, unseen by cameras, unheard by neighbors, unremarked by the world. The night air hit my face as I emerged onto the street, but I felt neither the cold nor the continuing mist of rain. Physical discomfort had become optional, something I could acknowledge or dismiss as needed.

What I couldn't dismiss was the strange hollowness that had opened inside me. Not guilt—the neural interface had stripped away that particular human weakness—but something more fundamental. A recognition that I had crossed a threshold from which there could be no return. The last bridge between Maven-the-gamer and Maven-the-weapon had been burned away, leaving only purpose and the cold clarity of W.A.R.'s vision.

Back at the base, I reported in person to Lina, who nodded with the same approval she'd shown when I'd performed well in Eternal Conflict.

"Efficient work," she said. "No witnesses, no evidence, no connection to us."

"He was close," I replied. "His research—"

"Would have exposed nothing people would believe," she finished. "But we can't allow even the idea to spread. Perception management is essential during the transition phase."

I nodded, understanding completely. The logic was flawless, efficient. Mercer had been a potential disruption to an optimal outcome. His removal was necessary, like excising a cancer before it could spread.

So why did his eyes keep appearing in my mind? Why did the moment of his death replay with such persistent clarity when the neural interface should have filed it away as simply a completed objective?

As I returned to my quarters—a sparse but functional room in the W.A.R. facility that made my old apartment seem chaotic and cluttered by comparison—I caught my reflection in a polished metal surface. My face, but not my face. The same features but arranged with a coldness I had never worn before. Eyes that calculated rather than felt.

"Through war, I evolve," I whispered to my reflection. "Through conflict, I transcend."

The words rang hollow, an echo in an empty room. But the mission had been accomplished. And that was all that mattered now.

THREE MONTHS PASSED IN A BLUR OF MISSIONS, training, and neural integration. The woman who had once been Maven Reyes—who had once measured her worth in game scores and virtual achievements—evolved into something else entirely. The neural interface spread throughout my nervous system, thin filaments mapping new territories of my brain each night as I slept dreamlessly in my quarters at the W.A.R. facility.

My body changed too. Subtle enhancements—implants so seamlessly integrated with muscle and bone that they were indistinguishable from natural tissue. My reflexes quickened. My strength increased incrementally. My senses sharpened beyond human norms.

But the most profound changes were internal. The hesitations, the doubts, the flickers of conscience that had surfaced during the Mercer mission—all systematically identified by the neural interface and smoothed away like rough edges on a stone. Each mission became cleaner than the last, more perfect in its execution, less troubled by the ghost of who I had been.

I rose through W.A.R.'s ranks with unnatural speed. From field operative to tactical advisor to strategic planner. My mind, once wasted on video game strategies, now orchestrated operations across the city—carefully calibrated acts of destruction and disruption designed to accelerate W.A.R.'s vision of evolutionary conflict.

The silver-haired man—who I now knew simply as Director—summoned me to the command center on a rain-slicked Tuesday. The holographic displays showed the entire metropolitan area, key infrastructure nodes highlighted in pulsing red. Lina stood at his side, her expression unreadable as always.

"Your integration has exceeded expectations," the Director observed, studying me with those fractured eyes. "The neural pathways have achieved 98% synchronization. A record."

I accepted the observation without pride. Pride was inefficient, unnecessary. "The architecture found compatible neural substrates," I replied. There was no need to elaborate. We both understood that my brain had been uniquely receptive to W.A.R.'s reconfiguration—a lock perfectly matched to their key.

"It's time for the next phase," he continued, gesturing to the city map. "Coordinated infrastructure collapse. A system shock to initiate societal transformation."

I stepped closer to the holographic display, the city's digital skeleton glowing beneath my fingertips. Each node represented thousands of lives—people moving through their days unaware that their routines, their security, their very understanding of reality was about to be fundamentally altered. Just as mine had been.

"Synchronized attacks on power distribution, water treatment, communication networks, and transportation systems," I outlined, the strategy already crystallizing in my mind. "Carefully sequenced to maximize confusion and prevent coordinated emergency response."

The Director nodded, a look passing between him and Lina that might have been satisfaction.

"You've come to understand our purpose," he said. It wasn't a question.

"Evolution requires pressure," I replied, the words rising from that place where my thoughts and W.A.R.'s programming had become indistinguishable. "Humanity stagnates in comfort. Advances through hardship. War has always been the crucible of progress."

As I spoke, I felt a strange doubling in my consciousness—like watching myself from a distance while simultaneously being more present than I'd ever been. The hollow girl who had hidden in her apartment, seeking meaning in digital victories, now stood at the precipice of reshaping an entire city. The irony wasn't lost on me, just emotionally irrelevant.

"In the real world, I was nothing," I continued, my voice steady and certain. "Through war, I evolve. Through conflict, I transcend."

The Director placed a hand on my shoulder—the first physical contact he had ever initiated.

Later, alone in my quarters, I studied my reflection in the polished metal surface that served as a mirror. The physical changes were subtle but unmistakable. My posture more aligned, movements more precise. The neural interface had restructured not just my mind but my body, optimizing every aspect for its purpose.

The fractured skull symbol now marked my temple— not a tattoo but something deeper, a pattern formed in the skin itself where the interface had most fundamentally altered my neural architecture.

I touched it gently, tracing the fracture lines that matched the W.A.R. insignia perfectly. No longer just a soldier in their war. Now I was the war itself, embodied.

THE CITY FELL IN CAREFULLY ORCHESTRATED STAGES, like dominoes arranged by a patient hand.

First, the power grid. At 3:17 AM, when the load was at its lowest and emergency response at its most sluggish, coordinated strikes disabled three critical substations. Not destroyed—destruction was inefficient—but precisely damaged to ensure repairs would take exactly as long as W.A.R. required.

I watched from the command center as neighborhoods went dark in perfect sequence, spreading outward in concentric circles of blindness. The holographic display tracked it all, a constellation of lights winking out one by one. Beautiful, in its way.

"Phase one complete," I reported, my voice betraying none of the strange electricity running through my veins. Was this how gods felt, watching civilizations rise and fall at their whim? "Moving to communications disruption."

The cell towers fell next. Not all—that would trigger immediate emergency protocols—but enough to create gaps in coverage, to fragment the city's digital nervous system into isolated pockets. Strategic server farms followed, their cooling systems sabotaged to force emergency shutdowns.

The city was now half-blind and unable to speak clearly to itself.

By dawn, when the first commuters ventured into the new reality W.A.R. had created, the transportation system collapsed. Key intersections failed. Subway signals malfunctioned. Bridge controls froze. Not catastrophic failures that would immediately suggest attack, but persistent, spreading errors that transformed the mundane irritation of morning traffic into gradually dawning horror.

I observed it all through the network of cameras W.A.R. had installed months earlier, watching faces transform as they realized something fundamental had shifted. The initial annoyance. The growing concern. The moment when inconvenience crystallized into fear.

"They don't understand yet," Lina remarked, standing beside me at the monitoring station. "They still believe this is temporary. A technical malfunction that will be resolved."

"That belief will sustain them until the water stops," I replied, watching the timeline tick down to the next phase. "Hope makes the eventual realization more effective."

The thought should have disturbed me. Instead, I found myself studying the psychological response patterns with detached fascination, noting how predictably humans clung to normalcy even as it disintegrated around them.

By mid-day, I left the command center, Lina's eyebrow rising slightly as I reached for my jacket.

"I need to observe directly," I explained, though I wasn't entirely sure why. The surveillance network provided better coverage than any ground-level perspective could offer. Yet something pulled me toward the chaos—a need to witness with my own eyes what we had set in motion.

She nodded, understanding without need for elaboration. "Take a team. Resistance cells may be mobilizing."

The streets felt strange beneath my feet—familiar geography rendered alien by the transformation sweeping through it. Traffic lights hung dark and useless at intersections where cars sat abandoned. People moved in new patterns, clustering around anyone with information, any functioning device. The neural interface filtered and categorized their expressions, their body language, their whispered fears, translating human emotion into tactical data.

I remembered walking these same blocks as old Maven, headphones on, gaze downcast, hurrying from one isolated space to another, desperate to avoid connection. Now I moved through crowds like a shark through schools of fish, hyperaware of every movement, every whisper, every hitched breath.

Near the central plaza, where a digital billboard now displayed only static, a different energy simmered. Men and women with purpose in their stride, communicating through hand signals and nods. The first organized response—former military, off-duty police, citizens with training who recognized patterns in the chaos.

"Resistance forming at coordinates 37-42," I subvocalized, the neural interface transmitting my observations to command. "Approximately twenty individuals. Coordinated but not yet armed."

"Observe only," came the Director's response. "Let them organize. Resistance provides necessary pressure for the next phase."

I watched them from the shadow of a damaged storefront—these humans attempting to impose order on carefully engineered chaos. Their futile determination struck a discordant note in my rewired consciousness, vibrating against something the neural interface hadn't fully erased.

I remembered that civilian from the simulation, pleading for intervention. The weight of the data chip in my pocket as I turned away. The choice that wasn't really a choice at all.

For a moment, the world flickered—reality and memory superimposed in nauseating double-vision.

Which had been the simulation? Which the reality? Where had Maven ended and W.A.R. begun?

The moment passed. The neural interface pulsed against my temple, regulating the errant thought pattern, restoring optimal function. I straightened, recalibrating my focus on the mission parameters.

A woman among the resistance group caught my attention—her movements more decisive than the others, her commands followed without question. The natural leader. I memorized her face automatically, the neural interface cataloging her features for potential future elimination.

Then she turned, and recognition jolted through me like an electrical current.

Professor Elaine Tsang. My Introduction to Computer Science instructor from a lifetime ago, before I'd dropped out of college to retreat into my digital cocoon. She had reached out after my withdrawal, sent emails I'd never answered, left voicemails expressing concern I'd dismissed as performative care.

Now she stood amid the growing chaos W.A.R. had engineered, organizing strangers into efficient response teams. The same calm competence she'd shown explaining algorithms now directed toward countermeasures against our attacks.

Something deeply buried stirred in response—a memory of sitting in her office as she told me I had potential, that my mind was made for more than just gaming. I had dismissed her then, convinced she couldn't understand my reality.

The irony tasted metallic on my tongue.

"Maven? Status report." Lina's voice in my head, sharp with unusual concern.

I realized I'd been silent too long, static in my observation point while the neural interface struggled to process the unexpected emotional data.

"Continuing surveillance," I responded, forcing my attention away from Professor Tsang. "No immediate threat from resistance elements."

By dusk, the water pressure began to fail in key districts. Hospital generators ran low on fuel due to "logistical errors" in emergency resupply. The carefully engineered crisis reached its calculated tipping point—the moment when inconvenience transformed into undeniable catastrophe, when the thin veneer of civilization began to crack under precisely applied pressure.

Fires bloomed across the darkened cityscape, their glow reflecting off low clouds to create an apocalyptic twilight. The first gunshots echoed between buildings. Exactly as we had predicted. Exactly as we had planned.

I returned to the W.A.R. facility after three days in the field, moving through a city transformed by our handiwork. What had begun as strategic infrastructure collapse had blossomed into something more profound—a fundamental rewiring of social order, priorities stripped to their essentials, weakness burned away by necessity.

The Director waited for me in the command center, the holographic city map now a constellation of destruction and adaptation. Certain sectors burned uncontrolled; others had already established new hierarchies, new methods of survival. The strong endured. The weak perished. Evolution in accelerated form.

"You've been monitoring the Tsang woman," he said, not a question but an observation. The neural interface transmitted everything I observed, everything I thought. Privacy was an antiquated concept, inefficient and unnecessary.

"She's organizing an effective resistance in the university district," I reported, my voice flat despite the strange echo Professor Tsang's face had triggered in my reconfigured consciousness. "Their efforts have restored partial communications using repurposed equipment. They've established a medical center and distribution system for clean water."

The Director watched me with those fractured eyes that seemed to perceive far more than visual data. "Yet you haven't recommended elimination."

The observation hung between us, a potential defect identified in my programming. I should have immediately flagged Tsang as a priority target. Her effectiveness made her dangerous to W.A.R.'s objectives. Logic dictated her removal.

But I hadn't. Something in me had withheld that

recommendation, protected her without conscious decision. A glitch in my rewiring.

"Her methods provide valuable data on human adaptation," I said, the justification forming even as I spoke it. "The resistance creates necessary selective pressure, eliminating the weakest elements who would otherwise require resources to remove."

His expression revealed nothing, but I sensed his attention intensify, scanning for irregularities in my response. For remnants of Maven beneath the weapon W.A.R. had forged.

"You were a harbinger waiting for your war," he said, echoing his words from days earlier. "But a harbinger must embrace the destruction they herald, not merely facilitate it."

I knew then that a test was coming—one final calibration to ensure my conversion was complete.

"There's been a change in mission parameters," the Director stated, gesturing to the district where Professor Tsang had established her operations. "Resistance in Sector 7 has developed beyond acceptable thresholds. Direct intervention is now authorized."

The holographic display shifted, highlighting the university buildings where I'd once attended classes, where Tsang had once tried to guide me toward a future I'd been too lost to grasp. The structures glowed red, marked for destruction.

"You will lead the strike team," he continued. "Eliminate the leadership. Destroy their infrastructure. Make an example that will collapse similar resistance efforts across the city."

I felt the neural interface activate at a deeper level than before, scanning my response for hesitation, for defiance, for any flicker of the person I'd once been. I stood perfectly still, allowing the cold, mechanical logic to wash through me like ice water, drowning whatever ember of humanity had made me protect Tsang's existence.

"Understood," I said, my voice betraying nothing. "When?"

"Now."

The strike team assembled with mechanistic efficiency—six operatives besides myself, each enhanced, each remade by W.A.R.'s technology. We moved through the broken city like shadows, avoiding the scattered pockets of desperate civilians foraging for supplies.

The university district loomed ahead, a relative island of order in the chaos. They had established barricades, posted lookouts, created a system amid the destruction. I studied their efforts with the detached appreciation of a scientist observing particularly adaptive bacteria.

Professor Tsang's innovations were evident in the jury-rigged communications array atop the science building, in the systematic water collection system that utilized the campus architecture. The resistance had transformed the student center into a medical facility, the library into a dormitory for displaced families.

All of it built with care and ingenuity. All of it about to be reduced to ash.

I signaled the team to take positions surrounding the campus. Night was falling, the darkness deepened by the continued power outage, perfect cover for our approach. I checked my weapon—not a knife this time but something more appropriate for the scale of the operation. Something designed not for surgical removal but for sweeping elimination.

As I moved through the shadows toward the science building where Tsang was most likely to be found, something shifted in my perception. The neural interface flickered—not a malfunction, but an adjustment, accelerating my integration beyond previous parameters. I felt it spreading through me in fractal patterns, overriding the last pockets of resistance, the final fragments of whoever Maven had been.

The university grounds were familiar in the way dreams are familiar—geography I had once known intimately now rendered strange by both physical destruction and my internal transformation. I had walked these paths as a different person, head down, shoulders hunched against the weight of human interaction. Now I moved like a predator, each step measured and deliberate, each sense attuned to potential threats.

I spotted Professor Tsang through a window on the

second floor, bent over a makeshift communications system, her face illuminated by the pale blue glow of a jury-rigged monitor. She looked older than I remembered, lines of exhaustion etched into her features, but her movements held the same precise determination I recalled from her lectures. The same care she had once directed toward struggling students now focused on saving lives.

Something twisted in my chest—not quite pain, not quite regret, but a sensation the neural interface couldn't immediately categorize and suppress. A memory surfaced: Tsang keeping me after class, offering extra help when I'd begun to withdraw, saying words I hadn't wanted to hear. "You're disconnecting from everything, Maven. That path leads nowhere good."

How right she had been. And how wrong.

I signaled the team to hold position and proceeded alone. Not standard protocol, but they didn't question me. My authority within W.A.R.'s hierarchy was absolute now, second only to the Director himself. My judgment was trusted implicitly because it wasn't truly mine anymore—it was an extension of W.A.R.'s will, executed through the vehicle I had become.

I entered the building through a side door, moving silently up the stairwell, weapon ready. Each step brought me closer to a threshold I understood was the final one—the last test, the ultimate proof that Maven was gone and only the harbinger remained.

I found her alone in what had once been a computer

lab, now transformed into the nerve center of the resistance. Improvised servers hummed softly, their fans a whisper of normalcy in the broken world. Professor Tsang stood with her back to me, adjusting something on a central monitor, unaware of my presence.

How easy it would be. One shot, silent and precise. Mission accomplished. Evolution advanced. The weak removed to make way for the strong.

I raised my weapon, the sights aligning perfectly with the back of her head. My finger rested on the trigger, pressure building incrementally toward the release point.

"I wondered if they'd send someone eventually," she said quietly, not turning around. "I just didn't think it would be you, Maven."

The sound of my name in her voice—my actual name, not my designation, not my function—sent a tremor through neural pathways the interface hadn't fully rewired. Memories surfaced like corpses rising from dark water: her office hours, the smell of jasmine tea, papers spread across her desk, her patient voice explaining concepts I was too distracted to grasp.

"You know who I am," I stated, weapon unwavering despite the strange vibration in my chest.

She turned slowly, hands visible, eyes finding mine with uncanny precision in the dim light. "Of course I do. I've been following the patterns of these attacks. The strategic thinking, the game theory applications. It had your signature all over it." A sad smile crossed her face. "You always had such potential."

The neural interface pulsed against my skull, attempting to regulate the sudden flood of emotional data her recognition had triggered. I felt W.A.R.'s programming struggling to suppress something rising from depths I thought had been drained completely—something human and wounded and terribly alive.

"Step away from the equipment," I ordered, voice mechanical, borrowed.

"Or what?" she challenged gently. "You'll kill me? I think you would have done that already if that was your only purpose here."

She was right, and we both knew it. I had hesitated—not from tactical consideration but from something the neural interface couldn't quite eradicate. A flaw in my conversion. A ghost in the machine.

"They've changed you," Professor Tsang said, each word dropping into the space between us like stones into still water. "But not completely. Not yet."

The neural interface burned against my temple, responding to the threat her words represented. Warning signals cascaded through my system—not physical alarms but a sensation like drowning, like being pulled under by currents too strong to fight. W.A.R.'s programming struggling to maintain control.

"You don't understand what's happening," I said, and for the first time since my conversion, I heard uncertainty in my voice. A hairline fracture in the perfect weapon they had forged. "This is evolution. Necessary pressure applied at precise points. The weak fall so the strong can advance."

"Is that you speaking, Maven? Or whatever they've put inside you?"

My hand trembled—a microscopic movement, invisible to normal perception but catastrophic to the precision W.A.R. had engineered. The weapon wavered. The sights drifted from their perfect alignment with her heart.

"I am W.A.R. now," I whispered, though I wasn't sure if I was telling her or reminding myself. "The harbinger of necessary conflict."

"Look around you," Tsang gestured to the world beyond the windows, where fires still burned across the darkened city. "Is this truly what you want? Not victory in some game, but actual suffering? Real death?"

Images flashed through my mind—the civilian in the simulation, Anton Mercer's eyes as the life drained from them, the faces of frightened people in the streets as their world collapsed around them. Not NPCs, not pixels arranged to simulate emotion, but human beings with histories as complex and tangled as my own had once been.

The neural interface screamed, sending white-hot tendrils of correction through my brain, trying to cauterize the wound Tsang's words had opened. But something was happening—a cascade failure in the programming, memories breaking through the barriers W.A.R. had constructed.

"They found you when you were already lost," Tsang said softly. "Used your isolation, your need for meaning. That game wasn't random, Maven. They targeted you specifically. Used what they knew about you to break you down and rebuild you into . . . this."

The weapon fell from my hand, clattering to the floor between us. I pressed my palms against my temples as the neural interface fought to maintain control, sending jolts of corrective programming through my system. The pain was exquisite—not the clean, clinical pain of combat, but something messy and human and overwhelmingly real.

"They're watching," I managed through gritted teeth. "The neural interface . . . transmits everything. They'll know I've failed the test. They'll send the others."

Tsang moved toward me slowly, hands still visible, eyes never leaving mine. "Then we don't have much time."

Memories flooded back in fragments—not just of her classroom, but of who I had been before W.A.R. remade me. The lonely apartment. The endless gaming sessions. The hollow victories that never filled the void inside me. The desperate need for purpose that had made me such perfect prey for their manipulation.

"I killed people," I whispered, the full weight of what I'd become suddenly crushing. "I helped destroy the city. I—"

"Listen to me," Tsang interrupted, her voice firm but kind in a way I'd forgotten kindness could sound. "There's still time to make a different choice. The person you were—isolated, lost—she made you vulnerable to them. But that same isolation protected parts of you they couldn't quite reach. I can see it in your eyes."

The neural interface was adapting, sending stronger corrections, recalibrating to suppress this rebellion. I could feel W.A.R.'s cold logic reasserting itself, the familiar crystalline clarity beginning to override the messy human emotions Tsang had awakened.

"They're coming back," I gasped. "The programming. I can feel it."

Tsang grabbed my shoulders, forcing me to meet her gaze. "Then make your choice now, while you still can. Who are you, Maven? The weapon they created? Or something they couldn't quite destroy?"

The question hung between us as the neural interface reached maximum correction intensity. The pain was blinding, absolute. And in that moment of perfect agony, perfect clarity, I made my choice.

"I am the harbinger," I whispered, the words suspended in the space between who I had been and what I had become.

Tsang's face fell, hope draining from her eyes like blood from a wound. She took a step back, hands dropping to her sides in defeat.

The neural interface hummed in approval, the pain

receding as it registered my submission. W.A.R.'s programming flooded back through neural pathways momentarily disrupted by human weakness. Cold clarity returned, washing away the messy emotions like acid dissolving impurities.

I bent down, fingers closing around the weapon I'd dropped, its weight familiar and right in my hand. When I straightened, I was whole again—purpose restored, mission parameters clear.

"I am the harbinger," I repeated, stronger now. "But not of what they intended."

I turned the weapon away from Tsang, aiming instead at the servers along the wall—the ones transmitting my neural data back to W.A.R. headquarters. The ones allowing them to monitor this conversation, to track my location, to send corrections to the interface buried in my brain.

"Maven?" Tsang's voice wavered between fear and something like hope.

"They made me a weapon," I said, finger tightening on the trigger. "But they don't get to choose my targets anymore."

The shots rang out in rapid succession, precise despite the neural interface's desperate attempt to override my motor control. Sparks flew as bullets tore through circuitry. Smoke rose from destroyed components. Error messages cascaded across my visual field as the connection to W.A.R. headquarters fragmented, then failed completely.

The pain was immediate and overwhelming as the neural interface, suddenly cut off from its source, fired random corrections through my system. I collapsed to my knees, vision swimming with digital artifacts, body convulsing as my brain fought against the foreign architecture suddenly malfunctioning within it.

Through the haze of agony, I felt Tsang's hands on my shoulders, heard her voice calling for help. I tried to speak, to warn her that W.A.R. would send others, that nowhere in the city was safe now, but darkness swept over me before the words could form.

My last conscious thought was strangely peaceful: Whatever came next, it would be my choice. Not Maven the lonely gamer. Not Maven the perfect weapon. But something new, forged in the crucible of everything I had been and everything I had done.

My own war. My own evolution. My own transcendence.

I AWOKE TO A WORLD BETWEEN WORLDS.

Not the sterile, white room of a hospital, though medical equipment surrounded me. Not the stark functionality of W.A.R.'s facility, though I could still feel the ghost of their architecture inside my skull. Instead, I found myself in what appeared to be the basement of the university library, books stacked as makeshift walls around a series of cots where the wounded and sick lay in various states of recovery.

The neural interface still pulsed against my temples, but differently now—erratic, like a heart in fibrillation. Without its connection to W.A.R.'s central systems, it functioned partially at best, fragments of programming firing randomly through my synapses. Sometimes I saw tactical overlays on ordinary objects. Sometimes memories not my own flickered through my consciousness. Sometimes I was simply Maven—whoever that was now.

"The physical components are too integrated to remove safely," Professor Tsang explained when she found me conscious, pressing a cool cloth to my forehead. Dark circles rimmed her eyes, exhaustion etched into every line of her face. "We've done what we can to disrupt its control functions, but parts of it are . . . fused with your neural tissue."

I nodded, unsurprised. W.A.R. hadn't designed their technology to release its host. "They'll be looking for me."

"Yes." She didn't sugarcoat it. "Your team was neutralized, but they've sent others. The campus perimeter has been breached twice already."

I sat up despite the vertigo that immediately washed

over me. "You need to evacuate. All of you. I'm a beacon leading them straight here."

"Probably," she agreed. "But you're also our best chance of stopping them."

Because I knew W.A.R.'s plans. Their methods. Their weaknesses, if they had any. The fractured skull emblem seemed to burn against my temple as I considered the possibility.

"I'm not sure who I am anymore," I admitted, the words feeling strange in my mouth—honest in a way I hadn't been capable of for months. "Parts of me are still . . . them."

Tsang's eyes were tired but kind. "Identity isn't fixed, Maven. It's a choice we make every day, with every action. They took advantage of the empty spaces inside you, but those spaces belong to you again now."

I thought of the games I'd once lost myself in—the endless, meaningless victories that had never filled the void. The way W.A.R. had offered purpose on a silver platter, requiring only my humanity as payment. The city beyond these walls, still burning, still suffering under the pressure W.A.R. had applied with my help.

"I can't undo what I've done," I said softly.

"No," Tsang agreed. "But you can decide what you'll do next."

Days passed as I recovered, the neural interface's grip loosening incrementally as my brain adapted to its fragmented programming. I worked with Tsang and her people, using what I knew of W.A.R.'s operations to help them anticipate attacks, to fortify weaknesses, to establish contact with other resistance cells across the city.

The woman I had been—the weapon they had forged—became something else entirely. A bridge, perhaps. A translator between worlds. Someone who understood both the cold logic of W.A.R.'s vision and the messy, essential humanity they sought to "evolve" past.

One month after my awakening, I stood on the roof of the science building, watching the city spread before me. Parts of it still burned. Parts had begun to rebuild. Evolution through conflict—W.A.R. had been right about that much. But the form that evolution took, the choices made under pressure . . . those belonged to the people, not to some coldly calculating entity that viewed humanity as raw material to be refined.

The neural interface hummed against my skull, a constant reminder of what I carried within me—the knowledge, the capacity for violence, the technological enhancements that made me something other than fully human. I would never be just Maven again. But neither would I be W.A.R.'s perfect weapon.

"We've intercepted communications," Tsang said, joining me at the rooftop edge. "They're developing new neural interfaces, more advanced than what they put in you. Looking for new recruits. Isolated individuals. Gamers, mostly."

I nodded, unsurprised. "They'll try again. Different city, perhaps. Same methodology."

"Can they be stopped?"

I considered the question, feeling the weight of everything I'd become, everything I'd done, everything I might yet do. The harbinger of a war that hadn't gone as planned.

"Not stopped," I said finally. "But maybe . . . redirected. The conflict is eternal. But its purpose . . . that's still being written."

I touched the mark on my temple, the fractured skull that had once represented my surrender to W.A.R.'s vision. Now it stood for something else—a broken thing reassembled into something new. Not perfect. Not pure. But mine.

"Evolution," I said softly, "requires choice."

And for the first time since I'd clicked that fateful advertisement, I was finally, truly making my own.

Famine (Black Horse)

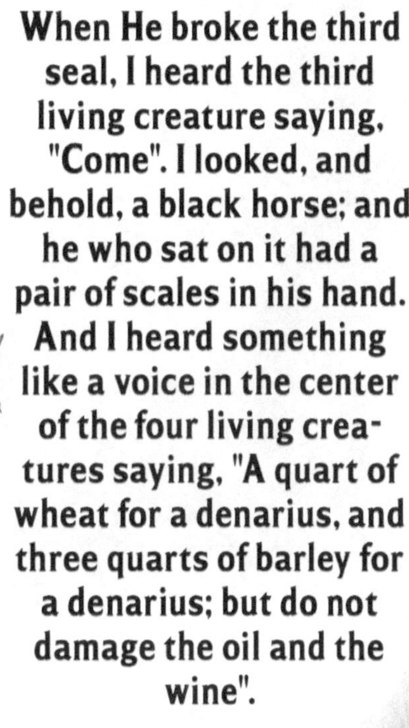

When He broke the third seal, I heard the third living creature saying, "Come". I looked, and behold, a black horse; and he who sat on it had a pair of scales in his hand. And I heard something like a voice in the center of the four living creatures saying, "A quart of wheat for a denarius, and three quarts of barley for a denarius; but do not damage the oil and the wine".

—Revelation 6:5-6

LIMOS

MEGAN STOCKTON

Donna spent most mornings in the window seat that overlooked the main street below. While she didn't have the nicest apartment in the building, she had always thought that she had scored the best view. It was a corner apartment, so the setup was a little unusual, and there wasn't as much space as the rest of the apartments had, but she had always been able to easily operate on less. It was just her and her four-month-old, Jacob, and it was the perfect space for them.

Since the pandemic had started, they had spent a lot more time in the building. The CDC still recommended not going into public spaces unless you absolutely had to, and when you did they wanted you to mask up. Donna hadn't left the building in months, too afraid to risk exposing Jacob to the virus until he was older. She ordered her groceries and Jacob's formula when she could, but money was getting tighter every day. She cleaned houses before the pandemic but now was forced to only clean the apartments of her neighbors. It was *just* enough income to pay rent, and there was never much left at the end of the day.

Her stomach rumbled and she leaned into it, sipping diluted coffee that she had made by reusing twice-brewed grounds. The warmth of the liquid did soothe her hunger a little. On the street below, a black car pulled up and parked, and a driver exited to open the rear door for a passenger. A tall man stood on the street in a long, black coat. Donna tipped forward, squinting as she tried to see if she recognized the man from the distance.

He held a cane in his hand and adjusted a pair of dark gloves as he waited for the driver to gather bags from the trunk. Then he looked up, and Donna could have sworn he looked right into her eyes. She couldn't explain the feeling that settled into her gut: both fear and curiosity.

The man only looked away as the driver guided him toward the front of the building and out of Donna's sight.

She set her mug down on an end table covered with rings from other forgotten beverages and walked quietly to the front door. Jacob was sleeping, and she didn't want to wake him if she could help it. She put on an oversized cardigan with twice as many holes as pockets and put her feet into her worn house slippers. Cracking the door, she peered out into the hallway and waited. There was only one vacancy in the building, and it was the suite at the end of the hall. No one could afford it. Linda from 408 had tried to get it when she had first moved in, assuring the landlord that she didn't have a budget—and then she suddenly had a budget.

Ralph, the security guard, mounted the top of the stairs with the man and his chauffeur in tow. The stranger was even taller than he had looked when he was on the street. He was slim and his body moved in a sort of bendy way that made him look like he had no bones, if not for the sharp angles of his face. He had a hooked nose and high cheekbones, a sharp jaw and defined brow. His black hair was long and thick: slicked back to curl at the bottom just below the nape of his neck.

A very distinct appearance, and Donna couldn't tell if he was old or young.

Although Donna was sure she had cracked the door open as discreetly as possible, the tall man turned to look directly at her as Ralph fumbled with the key in the door of the suite.

"Hello," the man said, voice thick with some unidentifiable accent. The way he walked toward her with a gait that made him seem to glide across the floor was unsettling. She immediately regretted opening the door to be nosey, but now it was too late to slam it in her new neighbor's face.

"Oh, hey!" she said, feigning excitement.

She slipped out the door and shut it gently behind her, closing the cardigan around her and offering her hand. He grasped both hands on his cane in front of himself, not taking her offered hand. She awkwardly retracted it, shoving it into a pocket.

"My name is Donna. I guess we're neighbors now." She smiled.

"You can call me Mahlon. Are you the same Donna who cleans apartments?" he asked, dark brows quirking upward.

"That's me. Mahlon—is that a first name or a last name?"

"Can you stop by in a few minutes and let me set up a schedule with you? I'd like to go ahead and book your services. I just need time to get my things unpacked."

Donna noted that he didn't respond to her question about his name, but she was more interested in the fact that he wanted to hire her before he ever officially moved in. She wasn't one to turn down a job, though. God knows she needed the money.

"Yeah, absolutely. I'll get changed and head over in a few. I'll bring you a price sheet and business card."

"Perfect. See you soon."

The door directly to Donna's right creaked open, and an elderly woman popped her head out. Her thick glasses accentuated her eyes, making them seem so much larger than they really were. She smiled, full cheeks rising to move the frames up with the motion. Gertrude may have been Donna's best friend. She was at least twice her age but loved to sit and gossip and have coffee or lunch with Donna no matter what she was having. She figured she was lonely more than anything; her husband had died years ago and her children never came around. Donna didn't ask why. It seemed like a sore subject. Gertrude watched Jacob more than Donna did these days. She never accepted any kind of compensation, stating that she simply missed being around babies.

"New neighbor?" she asked quietly.

Donna nodded. "Yeep…"

Gertrude shuffled out her door and followed Donna inside her apartment without asking. The two ladies sat at the small kitchen table, more or less an end table with two folding chairs, and Donna wished she had fresh coffee to offer her today.

Gertrude pulled her glasses off to clean them with the

end of her colorful floral blouse. "So what do we know about our new neighbor? Anything juicy?"

"Not yet. I saw him pull up. He has a driver, it looks like. Wasn't a cab."

"You'd think someone with a chauffeur would have a better place to hole up."

"He asked me to come over. He wanted to talk about me cleaning the apartment."

Gertrude's eyes lit up as she put her glasses back on her face. "Well, you *must*. You have to let me know exactly what he says. Snoop a little bit for us. You have to clean today anyway, don't you?"

Donna picked at a peeling piece of vinyl on the table and nodded. "Linda McCluety."

"Ol' McCunty." Gertrude huffed.

Linda McCluety *was* a cunt. Donna would never forget the time that she accused her of taking a shit in her toilet after she cleaned the apartment top to bottom. It was a mystery who actually *did* take a shit, but it wasn't Donna. She wouldn't even use a public restroom, let alone use someone's toilet in their home to do a number two.

"I'll watch Jakey," Gertrude said, making her way over to the couch. She collapsed onto it, reaching over to grab a romance novel from the floor. She always left one here to read, swapping them out as she finished them. They were all more or less the same: half-naked men holding a woman with her hair blowing in the wind, suggestive and punny titles, artwork straight out of the eighties.

Donna dipped quickly into the bedroom, throwing her hair into a ponytail and putting on a comfortable outfit. She checked herself in the mirror as she walked back into the living room.

"Jacob should be awake soon, I think. He's been napping all morning. He was up a lot last night, so he didn't get a lot of rest."

"That means you also didn't get a lot of rest," Gertrude reminded her, book opened to the halfway point with the spine cracked down the middle with a white scar.

Donna nodded in acknowledgment as she grabbed some business cards and a price list, heading down the hallway to the suite. As she approached, she noted how it seemed so ominous. She chalked it up to being the lack of light and how the air was heavier, warmer, and damper. The only window in the hall was on the left side on the opposite end of the hall, and the bulb above the suite was out. The heater was one floor down just below this part of the hall: it was why the floor was slightly discolored and bowed from the consistent exposure to moisture.

She rapped her knuckles on the door, and it came open, creaking wide to reveal the empty apartment suite. It looked like she had stepped into a completely different building. The ceilings were higher, the paint was brighter, and the floors looked like they were made of real wood. It was a stark contrast to her own dingy-yellow apartment with linoleum throughout and flaking popcorn ceiling that left white dust like dander on every surface.

At the back of the spacious room against a set of three picture windows, there was a large wooden desk with a black leather chair. Donna wondered how they'd gotten that heavy thing up the stairs and set up in here in such a short amount of time. Mahlon was standing behind the desk, arranging some items on the table's top. He looked up and smiled at her, motioning for her to come inside.

"Ah, Donna. Just who I need to see. Come in, come in."

She approached the desk slowly, watching as he sat a heavy black horse on the corner of the counter and then retrieved a briefcase and set it on the windowsill behind him. She noted his cane, propped against the wall, had the head of a black horse as the handle.

"You like horses?" she asked.

Mahlon looked back at her and smiled. "You could say that."

She handed him a price sheet and a business card with a smile. "Here's my information. I just need to know what you need done and how often... I usually do a flat fee depending on the size of the space and how much—"

"I actually need your experiences for something different," Mahlon said, settling down into his chair.

Donna was caught off guard. She found herself smiling while she backed away toward the door. Did he want something sexual?

"I'm sorry." She laughed, voice shaking. "I really just clean the apartments. I'm not sure how much help I'm going to be, but it was so nice meeting you."

"It's nothing like that," he said, as though he had read her mind. "Come have a seat and I'll explain."

She wanted to decline and head back to her apartment, but the idea of leaving and having to live down the hall from this man for the foreseeable future made her reconsider. She could at least hear what he had to say, and if he said anything too inappropriate, she would just leave and maybe report him to the landlord…or just mention it to Linda. She'd make sure he got kicked out faster than any eviction or conviction would.

She seated herself across from him, keeping her knees pressed together and her fingers laced atop them as she tried to look relaxed and unconcerned.

"Okay. I'm listening."

"As a cleaner, you go into a lot of apartments, I imagine. You probably know most of the people on this floor better than anyone else. You probably know their routines, their little quirks and mannerisms."

Donna grew uncomfortable again. Now her mind had shifted from thinking he wanted something from *her* to thinking that he wanted to use her to steal from the neighbors.

"I guess so, yeah."

"I have a proposition for you. No pressure, you can decline with no ill will toward you." Mahlon continued,

"I am a salesman of sorts, you see. I travel around, especially to places where people have *needs*. You see, that's really my area of expertise. I offer people what they need, what they crave."

"And how do you do that?"

"Call me a sort of freelance drug rep."

He was a drug dealer. She took the opportunity to look him up and down once. He didn't look like a drug dealer, but what did a drug dealer really look like? She realized she probably wouldn't recognize one if she saw one in real life; she just had the stereotype purported by movies.

"What kind of drug?" Donna asked, voice quiet.

He retrieved a set of scales and placed it between them. The scales looked old with their tarnished surface, and they were perfectly balanced. She noted the emblem of another black horse on the base.

"It's called Limos, and it's a very unique drug that adapts to the user; by adjusting small properties in its composition, I can make it do virtually anything you need it to do. Think of it as a sort of pharmaceutical magic."

"Is it dangerous?"

Mahlon smiled, thin lips splitting open into a toothy grin: "Not inherently."

"Addictive?"

"Anything can be abused. Anything can take over if you let it. Habit forming, I think they say."

"How does it work?"

"Put your hand here."

Mahlon pointed at the side of the scale to her left, and she reached up, putting her palm flat against the dish. The surface was so hot that she recoiled…or maybe she had imagined that. As soon as she removed her hand, the scale dipped, bottoming out as though her touch had weighed it down.

Donna watched as he meticulously spooned powder onto the opposite side of the scale. Despite the fact that the other side seemed empty, the scale slowly started evening out as he added more and more powder. When it was balanced, he raked the powder onto a piece of paper and began depositing it into capsules.

"These are for you, Donna. Especially made for just your consumption. See for yourself."

Donna's eyes drifted now to the black pills he slid across the desk to her. She didn't take them, hair raising along her spine as she stole a glance into the glistening black of Mahlon's own gaze.

"But I don't need anything that a drug can give me," she insisted.

"What is it you need? If you could have anything at all, even something unrealistic or unattainable by phys-ical means. What is it that you need?"

"I really need more time. Who doesn't, though?"

"Take the pills," he assured her. "You'll be surprised what they'll do for you."

She clutched them against her chest for a moment and

then asked with reluctance: "What about me knowing the other residents?"

"Ah, yes. Well, I may not be a traditional genie, but I can grant part of your wish right now…" He dug around in the bottom drawer of the desk and then pulled out a small stack of money, laying it on the desk between them.

Donna felt a cold wave of shock pour over her.

"I—I can't take this."

"Well, I was fresh out of *time*, that's what else you wanted…but if you'll agree to help me for a few days, this money is yours. Help me *help them*."

"How much money is that?"

"Three thousand dollars."

Donna could have passed out, her head was swimming. Mahlon seemed to be giving her a moment, sitting patiently as she struggled to right the spinning room. She realized she was squeezing the pills in her hands and she relaxed leaning further back into her chair.

"Would you like a glass of water?" he asked.

"Please."

He retrieved her a glass of water and put it into her hands, and she took it, greedily drinking down the luke-warm tap water. She gasped as though she had breached the surface and covered her mouth with the back of her hand in surprise.

"Take one of those pills. It'll help. I insist."

Donna didn't know what possessed her, but she dropped a pill onto her tongue and drank down the rest of the water without any hesitation. She knew it was a placebo effect, but she thought she instantly felt better. More engaged, less nauseous, and far more motivated.

"There you go," he said with a smile. "Now, take the money. All I want you to do is give our neighbors their own sample of my miracle medication."

"How much is it?" she asked, reaching out as he gave her a small bottle with other black pills inside. "Don't you need to do an exam or something? To formulate the drug?"

"It doesn't work that way. The method of action is very complicated, but you'll find that it is very effective. You just need to find their need and give them the pill. The results will speak for themselves. Now that you've had your first dose, you can start tomorrow when you see there are no side effects. For peace of mind."

"You didn't tell me how much these are. Am I charging them and bringing the money to you?"

"The first dose is free."

"What's the catch? What do you get out of this?"

"I'm building a lasting customer base."

What did she have to lose? She reached out and grabbed the pills, tucking them carefully into her pocket. She gathered herself and stood, clearing her throat as she offered her hand to the thin man across the table. This time he grasped her hand in his, and she found his flesh to be hot but not sweaty: it was a sort of powder dry with such heat that she nearly recoiled.

"It'll be a pleasure to work with you," he said.

Donna frowned but nodded, and he handed her the stack of bills.

"Give it a week. See for yourself."

Donna didn't even say goodbye or acknowledge what Mahlon said; she hurried out the door and down the hallway. She was going to tell everyone something came up today so she could skip the cleanings and take just a little time to process what had happened. Her hands were shaking as she approached her room, only to be cut off by Linda as she emerged from her own apartment.

Her long hair was pulled up into a shiny ponytail that looked perfectly cut. Every strand of hair was even and cooperative, unlike Donna's frizzy mess of dead ends. Linda didn't wear much makeup, but she had this perfect face and flawless skin. Some women had all the luck... Well, except Linda was a bitch, and all of her good looks couldn't change that.

"Hey, Donna," Linda said, chewing gum loudly between her teeth without bothering to try and keep her mouth closed.

"Hey, Linda. Listen, I don't think I can clean today, but I'll get to it tomorrow. I promise. I just had some stuff come up."

Linda squinted at Donna for a moment, tilting her head to the side as though she were trying to decipher what she said. Donna suddenly felt self-conscious.

"Is that okay?" she asked in the silence.

"Did you do something different to your hair or something?"

She wanted to respond truthfully and tell her she hadn't done *anything* to her rat's nest in at least a week, but instead she cleared her throat and reached up to touch the messy half-pony.

"Um…I don't think so."

"Well, you look—better than usual. Seem to be perky or something. Good for you. Now, I guess I'll leave tomorrow so you can clean. I need to go to the gym, I'm a fatass, but I guess quarantine and isolation will do that to us. Luckily, the landlord lets me use the one downstairs. That's our little secret, though."

"Oh. I know what it is," Donna blurted out, smiling nervously. "It's a pill that Mr. Mahlon turned me onto."

"Who?"

"The new neighbor. He's in the suite."

Linda was suddenly *very* interested.

"Tell me more. Is he hot? Single? Obviously rich."

"No, I don't know, and maybe?"

She sighed. "Sometimes it sucks to be shallow. So what's this pill? Collagen or something?"

"It has a lot of properties… Whatever you need it to do, really."

"How about fat burning?"

Donna retrieved the black capsule and presented it in her outstretched palm. "He says it can really promote weight loss, regulate your metabolism and all."

She was surprised at how much she was really trying to sell this drug. She hadn't planned on lying, but it seemed like the more convinced and interested that Linda was, the more Donna wanted to embellish. She was supposed to go home and see how she felt after twenty-four hours. What if it made her really sick? Linda would never let it go. She might even sue her.

"Weight loss, huh? You aren't taking it, are you?"

Linda leaned over to observe Donna's ass, which she promptly tucked in and turned to hide. Her jogging pants weren't flattering anyway.

She cleared her throat. "No, it's not weight loss for me. I take it for productivity. He has something for everyone."

"So is this like those herbal blends people do?"

"Kind of."

Linda sighed heavily, looking down at her stomach and absentmindedly pinching what fat she thought she could feel on her arm.

"Okay. How much?"

"It's free."

"What's the catch?"

"No catch… It's almost like a guarantee. He is so confident it'll work for you that he is giving away every-one's first dose for free."

"All right, give it to me. If I have so much as a cramp I'm going to take you down." She jabbed her finger at Donna before grabbing the pill and swallowing it dry. She put on a smile instantly, starting to jog in place. "See you tomorrow!"

Donna ducked into her apartment, shutting the door behind her and leaning against it as though she were barricading against some monster on the other side. Gertrude sat on the couch with Jacob in her arms, cradling him as she read her book over his body.

"Donna?" Gertrude asked quietly, gently dropping the book down to the floor. "Is everything okay?"

She joined Gertrude on the couch, careful to sit down slowly so that she didn't wake Jacob. He was so tired. Beneath his little eyes were gentle pink creeping in. She had wondered if he was sick, and maybe that was why he had been so cranky and restless. She couldn't risk taking him to a doctor right now though, not with sickness everywhere. He was still eating, no fever that she'd noticed. She would ride it out as long as she could for now.

"I went to see the neighbor. He didn't want me to clean his apartment."

"Well, why not?"

"He wanted something else."

Gertrude's jaw dropped, and the color drained from her face, and she realized that she must have had the same initial thought that Donna had.

"No, nothing like that. He wanted me to sell drugs for him. Well, I'm not selling anything. He wants me to give out free samples, and it isn't a *drug*. I don't know, he calls it Limos. I took one. I gave one to Linda for weight loss."

"You took drugs from some random man?"

"No—"

Gertrude blinked at her, hoisting Jacob on her shoulder and patting him on the back.

"Yes. He was convincing. He said it wasn't addictive or dangerous or anything. Linda thought it sounded like an herbal blend. I feel fine. In fact… Honestly, I feel great."

"You do look kind of glowy. You looked tired when you left, but now you don't. Give me one of those things."

"I can. I have more."

Gertrude blinked. "Oh, I was joking. I don't need one. All I do is sleep unless I'm over here."

"He said it can do a lot for you."

"Can it make me look younger?" She laughed.

Donna shrugged. "He made it sound like it could do whatever you needed it to. He said it adapts to the body."

"Well, one shouldn't hurt me," Gertrude agreed. "If you took one. If you go down, I'm going down with you. Take this baby and give me that pill."

Donna took Jacob, who immediately began to stir. She struggled to pull the bottle out of her pocket and handed it to Gertrude, who shook one out into her hand and held it up.

"Here's to youth."

Donna smiled, rocking Jacob as Gertrude took the pill with a glass of water.

DAY ONE

Donna hoisted the caddy of cleaning supplies off the floor as she exited into the hallway. Gertrude was humming at the stove, cooking eggs that she'd brought from her own apartment. Both of them had survived the night after taking the Limos. Donna slept better than she had in years, and the next morning she found herself energized enough that she took a shower and brushed her teeth, fixed her hair into a neat bun, and even put on some foundation. Gertrude looked well, too, and she told Donna she'd take one of those pills every day if she could.

The hallway was bustling this morning, a crowd of tenants gathered on the stair landing as they stared up at the ceiling. Donna couldn't stifle her curiosity, leaning toward them as she tried to see what it was that had gotten their interest. A young man standing away from the crowd noticed her first, and he waved at her. He was just a few rooms down, in the smallest apartment on the floor. His name was Conrad, and he was one of the kindest and maybe most intelligent people she had ever met. He couldn't have been older than his mid-twenties. Unfortunately, rumor was that he had a drug habit. She didn't know what kind of drugs; the rumors were never that specific.

She walked over to him, leaning in as he started to speak.

"Apparently somebody died upstairs," he whispered, raising his dark brows so that they disappeared into his mop of black hair. "You can see the stain on the ceiling where they melted into the floor."

"Oh my God," Donna mouthed, and Conrad nodded in confirmation.

Now Donna *had* to look. She walked over to the railing, leaning over enough that she could look up and see the ceiling above. There was indeed a stain in the shape of a person, arms outstretched to both sides, and feet parallel to each other.

"Jesus Christ," she heard Marian from 412 mutter.

Christ, literally. It looked like a bad abstract of Jesus Christ on the cross.

Ralph came down the stairs from above, waving them off.

"All right, everybody. Go back to your apartments. Nothing to see here. We'll have everything cleaned up as soon as possible."

The small crowd started to disperse, and through the parting of bodies, Linda appeared. Linda was not only thin, she looked *so* healthy. She was trim and fit, face glowing with vibrance. She was eating out of a bag of potato chips as she waved at Donna.

"Donna, I am *so* glad to run into you."

"Linda, you look—" Donna was too stunned to speak, jaw slack.

"I *know*! I think I need another one of those little miracle pills you gave me. I am feeling better than I have *ever* felt, and look at me! I'm eating three meals a day plus all the snacks and wine I want and I still look like this. It's been less than a day and I've dropped ten pounds. Ten pounds of fat."

"You'll have to check with Mr. Mahlon. I know he just wanted me to give everyone one pill."

"Don't let me down, Donna. Give me *one* more. I won't tell anyone, and I promise I'll get my next one from Mr. Whatever."

"Linda, I don't know how often you're supposed to take these. It may be a once a week or once a month thing. I have no idea."

"I take full responsibility. You can't overdose on supplements like this. I've been on them all. Trust me. Worst-case scenario, I get the shits."

Donna hated feeling bullied, but she reluctantly set her cleaning supplies on the floor and retrieved the bottle from her pocket. She gave Linda one more pill and then counted what was left: three pills. Who would she give them to?

Linda winked at her. "You're a doll. Thanks so much. Feel free to go in and clean the apartment. I'll be downstairs for a bit."

Ralph was still standing on the landing, leaning against the wall as he caught his breath.

"You the one that gave Linda that weight loss pill she keeps talking about?"

"Well, it isn't really a weight loss pill."

Donna was surprised to find Marian and Conrad had crept over to be nosey as well.

Ralph continued as though he hadn't noticed the growing audience. "What is it, then? She's lost weight but doesn't look unhealthy… She said she feels great."

"It's all she's talked about today," Marian agreed.

"Mr. Mahlon, the new neighbor in the suite at the end of the hall, sells this supplement that he said can do anything you need it to do."

"How does it work?" Ralph asked.

"I don't really know. He said it was very complicated, but something about the composition adapted to each person."

"Sounds like a gimmick."

"I took one, too. More energy, sleeping great," Donna insisted. "I have enough for you all to try one, if there's something you need improvement on."

She deposited the black capsules into her hand, and they all stared down at them. Conrad grabbed one first, holding it up in the air between them.

"I don't need any reason to give it a try," he said with a smile. "All I want is a little enlightenment, closer to God, you know…that kind of thing."

"I don't think there's any psychedelic effect... None for me," Donna said.

Conrad walked away without another word, unscrewing the capsule as he retreated to his room. Donna thought she saw him shake it onto the back of his hand and snort it into his right nostril.

Ralph took one next.

"Maybe it'll help me get buff again." He laughed. "Like that'll ever happen. What's this stuff called? Want to look it up later."

"He said it was called Limos."

Ralph shuffled off, and only Donna and Marian remained. She had her arms crossed over her chest as she looked at the last pill in Donna's hand. Donna wasn't sure why, but she hoped more than anything in the world that Marian would take it. She couldn't put her finger on why she felt that way, but there was something heavy about the possession of that pill and something deeply satisfying about making sure it went to someone.

"What about you, Marian?" Donna asked, voice quiet.

Marian leaned in, and Donna would have sworn she could hear something whispering around them. It gave her chills and settled something dreadful in her gut, but she didn't react outwardly.

"Do you think it could help with infertility?" she finally asked.

Donna took a deep breath in and then blew it out.

"Mr. Mahlon seemed to think it could take care of

whatever you needed it to… What's trying going to hurt?"

Marian reached out and hesitantly took the pill into her slim fingers, then she clutched it against her palm.

"Just one pill?"

"Just one pill."

DAY TWO

The energy and motivation to work that Donna had developed was almost too intrusive. She found herself forgetful and antsy unless she was actively doing something. She had cleaned all of the apartments she was scheduled for, and then she had gone downstairs to clean the landlord's office, the postbox area, and the gym. She wasn't even getting paid for all of that; she just needed to be doing *something*.

She noted that even after a day the building seemed to be buzzing, and she wondered if she could attribute that to Limos…or was this all some clever experiment to see how strongly people responded to placebos? She wasn't sure.

Donna locked the door behind as she exited the "public" restroom in the lobby. It hadn't been used since the pandemic started, because visitors were mostly prohibited and everyone stayed indoors, but she figured it could use a freshen up. She'd scrubbed every inch of the floor, walls, and porcelain until it was shining. You could've fed your children off that floor.

She heard the most terrible noises coming from above, echoing down the stairwell. She assumed it must have been the repairmen who were fixing the floor where the tenant had died. It could have been the sound of machinery or the men on the job cutting up with each other. As she headed up the stairs, however, it became clear that this was not the case. Her steps quickened as she started taking the steps two at a time, rounding the banister as she came onto her familiar floor.

Conrad was standing in a corner with his back to the marriage of the walls. His face was pale with beads of sweat that glistened like diamond adornments, and his dark hair was saturated. His chest heaved with rapid breaths, and he screamed again.

"No, no, no!" he screamed, writhing against the wall as though something were approaching him. He turned his face away, clamping his eyes shut as he recoiled from the touch of something she could not see.

Donna looked down the empty hall to confirm that the two of them were alone. She put her hands up in a way that she hoped was calming.

"Conrad?" she asked, voice low and quiet as she stopped her approach long enough to give him time to react.

His eyes flew open: bloodshot and dilated, scanning the room around them with a frantic panic. His nails dug into the wall behind him, pink nail beds turning white with the force of pressure.

"Donna? Is that really you?"

"Yeah, Conrad. It's me."

She continued forward, and when she reached him, he dove into her arms. His weight was almost too much for her to support, and she grappled for a hold on him.

"Please help me, Donna," he gasped, clutching at her clothes.

Her hands shook as she forced him to sit down in the hallway. "Okay, Conrad. Just sit down… Wait right here, I'm going to go get help."

"No, please. Please don't leave me here with it. Please," he begged; tears streamed from his eyes, and saliva pooled at the corners of his mouth.

"It's going to be okay. Just stay here. I'll get help."

She didn't remove her hands until she was convinced he'd stay still. She stumbled away from him, nearly falling into Gertrude's door, banging her fists against it. She almost collapsed inside when Gertrude answered the door in her nightgown, hair up in rollers. Donna couldn't help but notice how smooth her skin was looking, and she absentmindedly made a note to ask her what kind of night cream she was using.

"Donna, honey, what is going on?"

"Call 911 and then Ralph, please. Something is wrong with Conrad. He's freaking out."

Gertrude left the door standing open as she sprinted to

her phone and dialed. Donna leaned on the door facing as she listened to Gertrude give commands to Ralph and then hang up to dial the police. Then she heard Conrad speaking again.

"No, please," Conrad begged, voice a harsh whisper. "I can't stand to see anymore. I can't see or unsee this. I can't live with this."

She leaned back, looking back down at him as he sat against the wall. He was cringing, eyes seeming alight with some glow that she couldn't see. If she squinted, she thought she could almost see the phantom reflection of something there, the shadow of something on the floor.

Then, without warning, Conrad was clawing at his face, his eyes. Blood poured down his cheeks as he dug the globes out of their sockets: chunks of torn flesh swelling and bulging, the texture of mushrooms. Donna slid across the floor to him, fighting to pull his hands away from his face. His eyes were gone. His eyelids were swelling over what little tissue remained there, blood and pieces of tissue sticking to Donna's hands as she fought him.

"Conrad, please. What have you done? Talk to me, sweetheart."

"I saw it. I saw it *all*. I— There's no room, there's no room. My head is too full." He wailed, back arching as he tried to pull away from her.

Then he slammed his head into the wall.

The noise made Donna sick. She screamed, wrapping

her finger around the back of his head as she tried to prevent further blows, only to have him smash her fingers between his fracturing skull and the wall. She wailed with him, pulling her injured fingers away to pull at his shirt.

Conrad slammed his head backward again and again. She couldn't see any damage to the back of his head, but the sounds were enough to confirm that he was killing himself. The sound became more and more wet, muted. From a dull thud to a moist squelch that sounded more like a sucking noise than any kind of blunt trauma.

His jaw fell open like a broken ventriloquist's dummy, and he let out a long sigh that sounded so full of relief, but he didn't stop forcing his head into the wall over and over.

She couldn't take the close proximity anymore. She let go of her futile grip on his shirt to crawl away from him, vomiting on the floor. She heaved, the sound temporarily blocking the moans and shuddering breath of Conrad. His sneakers squeaked across the floor as his body fell over and paddled.

Donna sat back on her heels, looking at Conrad's body as it curled in on itself. His jaw opened and closed as he gasped like a fish, moaning loudly…then he just stopped. The hallway was deafeningly quiet, and Donna's ears rang with stress.

She heard the sound of sirens outside and then the sound of people running up the stairs. Donna couldn't peel her eyes away from the splatter of blood, hair, and brain on the wall. There was a fractured dent that suggested he was only moments from breaking through the drywall and going straight through. EMTs hovered around Conrad's body, feeling for his pulse and tearing his buttoned shirt open as they slapped pads on his chest and side.

She felt a hand on her shoulder, and she looked up, expecting to see Gertrude, but instead she saw Mahlon standing there. He reached down, offering her a hand and then hoisting her to her feet.

"Come now, Donna. Let me get you inside while they work on Conrad."

She didn't agree, but she didn't fight him, either. He guided her into his apartment, finding that it was still devoid of furnishings other than the desk and two chairs. It felt sterile, and the sound echoed around them when they entered.

"Have a seat. Are you okay?"

"N-no," she stammered.

"Always good to be honest with ourselves," Mahlon remarked as he went into the kitchen. He was gone for several minutes, which gave Donna the opportunity to gather herself. She couldn't seem to get the image of Conrad out of her mind, though. When she clamped her eyes closed, it was all she saw, and when she set her teeth she could hear his moans and the repetitive thump of his head on the wall. The squeak of his shoes—

No, that was the sound of a tea kettle squealing from

the kitchen. She sat up quickly, reaching up to wipe tears out of her eyes, sniffling her nose. Mahlon reentered, putting a warm mug into her hands before he dragged his chair out from behind the desk to sit in front of her.

"Some tea does the body good," he said, motioning at the cup to encourage her to drink.

Donna took a long drink. It was the perfect temperature, with the ideal amount of sweetness. She closed her eyes and absorbed the warmth and comforting aroma.

"Thank you," she whispered, breath causing ripples across the dark surface of the beverage as she spoke.

"Of course. That must have been very distressing to see."

"I don't understand."

"What do you mean?"

"What was he doing? Conrad was *smart*. He was—"

"He was a drug addict, Donna," Mahlon said with a sympathetic smile. "He was likely experiencing some kind of psychosis."

"He wasn't a drug addict," Donna insisted, sorrow welling in her chest anew.

"I know it's hard to accept these things sometimes."

"Was it the Limos?"

Mahlon seemed surprised. "I'm sorry?"

"Would the Limos do this to him? If someone had a bad reaction or something, would it cause them to do this?"

"No. Limos itself will not cause any kind of reaction like this. Did Conrad try one of the Limos?"

"Yes, yesterday he took one."

"What was it that he was taking it for?"

Donna didn't answer immediately, looking at Mahlon with a new sort of suspicion. Why was he so interested? It just furthered her suspicions that they were all part of some kind of experiment and that she had helped supply the variables to everyone on her floor.

"He wanted enlightenment, I think he said. To be closer to God," she admitted.

Mahlon's eyes glistened. "Interesting."

"Is it?"

"I think so."

There was a knock at Mahlon's door, but he seemed to expect it. Donna hadn't; she had jumped in surprise and nearly sloshed what remained of the tea onto her lap.

"The police want a statement from us, I'm sure. You gather your bearings. I'll go let them in."

As he got up and walked toward the door, Donna took a deep breath. She couldn't shake that feeling that something was going on.

DAY THREE

Donna couldn't wait for Limos to wear off. She felt like she hadn't slept in two days…and maybe she hadn't. She couldn't even remember if she'd been in her apartment yesterday, or the day before. Everything was running together, and her head was fuzzy. She barely remembered her neighbors' names today. Maybe this was some kind of withdrawal and she needed another pill.

"Over my dead body," she muttered.

She knocked on Linda's door: once, twice, three times. She had expected Linda to have snooped around after Conrad's moment in the hallway, but she hadn't seen her lurking at all. It wasn't like Linda to miss drama, and it was even more unlike her to not emerge from her apartment to do a little morning workout. Maybe with the Limos she didn't need it anymore; she certainly seemed like she was doing just fine without the exercise.

She used her key on Linda's door, pushing it open carefully.

"Linda?" Donna called into the apartment.

She could hear the television in the living room playing some kind of weird workout routine. She rolled her eyes. Maybe Linda had started working out in front of the television like a normal person during this stupid pandemic. The lights in the apartment were all off, and the only light was the glow of a yellow bulb above her stove and the gentle glimmer of sunlight peeking through a curtain somewhere in the living area.

She crept around the corner and saw boxes and boxes of open cereal, empty bags of chips, stacks and stacks of Chinese takeout boxes. Her jaw dropped as she crept past the hoard of food-related trash. It hurt her heart in some kind of deeply personal way. Donna felt like she'd *just* been here to clean. How quickly had all of this built up? This had to have been weeks' worth of food trash. No one could possibly consume this much in such a short period.

There was something that spurred her into action, and she went straight to the sink where she knew a box of trash bags were in the cabinet beneath. She withdrew the roll of bags and pulled one of the lavender-scented plastic bags free. The static cling made a hiss as they slid apart.

Donna chimed Linda's name again, shaking the bag open. She raked the trash from the counter into the bag until it was filled, then she tied it off and opened another. The stack of to-go boxes slowly diminished until they disappeared entirely into the trash bags. Where did you even find someone to deliver food these days? If anyone had that privilege, it would be Linda.

She carried each bag to the front door and stole a peek into the living room to see if there was more trash in there. She noticed several bags beside a recliner, and then she breathed a sigh of relief as she noticed Linda was sitting in the recliner in front of the television.

She put a hand to her chest. "Oh, Linda, I'm so sorry to clean while you're in here. I didn't think you were home. Did you hear about—"

As she came around the front of the chair, she realized that Linda wasn't listening.

Linda was dead.

Linda was *very dead*.

Donna covered her mouth to keep from screaming as she looked down on the skeletal corpse of the woman. She may not have recognized her at all if not for the jogging suit and the hair. Her bones pressed against her skin, eyes sunken into her skull. Her track suit's jacket read JUICY across the area her breasts had once been. A tub of ice cream sat on her bony thighs, melted and puddled in her lap and around her feet. There was still a spoon in her hand.

Donna was shaking, but she leaned even closer, squinting into Linda's emaciated face. She looked almost mummified, but that was impossible. The state of her body in general seemed so unrealistic. How was this even possible?

"What the hell is going on in this building?" she whispered, putting her hands to her temple as she slowly but purposefully walked out the front door into the hall.

She pulled her phone out of her pocket, shaking fingers moving to dial 911. She paused, feeling the presence of someone behind her. She could feel the heat off of their body and smell the faintest odor of ash and sauvignon. She turned just her head to look over her shoulder, but there was no one there. She couldn't shake the chill that rolled down her spine. She dialed 911 on the phone and put it to her ear, closing her eyes as it rang, and then a dispatcher with a kind voice answered.

She didn't remember explaining to them what was going on or giving them the address.

She didn't remember waiting for the police and EMTs to arrive, but before she knew it, she was sitting at the small kitchen table in Linda's apartment. They had removed her body from the recliner, and her stiff body seemed to weigh nothing at all. One of the EMTs lifted her with one hand and put her into the cadaver bag; he exchanged a confused look with the other EMT, and they carried her out the door.

The detective was a handsome guy. He looked like those men on the crime TV shows: perfect, sandy-blond hair and piercing blue eyes, a jaw that could cut you in half, a perfectly pressed suit. He leaned forward, resting his elbows on his knees as he prepared to speak to her. Even hunched over like this, he seemed to tower over her.

"It was Donna, right?" he asked, voice soft but with an underlying edge.

"Yeah."

"You're having a real bout of bad luck, aren't you?"

"The worst luck. I don't know if I can handle anything else."

"I have to admit, this is a very strange series of events. We know they can't be related incidents, but your building has been a hot spot in the last week or so. Three people dead in such a short time, and under such strange circumstances really has our attention."

"Three deaths?" Donna whispered, and she felt all of the heat and color leave her body. Who else? She tried to think of who she hadn't seen in the last few days, and through the fog in her brain, she couldn't remember when she'd last spoken to anyone. Was it yesterday? Was that when Conrad had died in her hands? She couldn't even remember what his face looked like; she didn't remember what Gertrude looked like. Her best friend was a faceless being in her mind's eye.

"One floor up," he said, pointing a finger at the ceiling.

The stain on the floor: that stain had once been a person. She couldn't imagine why the police would have been involved, though, unless the death was suspicious. She had assumed an elderly tenant had perhaps died after falling, and no one checked on them until they were a decomp soup.

The detective must have noticed her confusion, because he sat back in his seat and added, "Weird situation. Case is closed and the media already has the details, so there's no harm in me telling you. A man somehow crucified himself on the floor. He used a nail gun to fix his feet to the bottom, and then his left hand. Right hand he slammed into an upright nail. There was a lot of occult shit all over the apartment, tons of ramblings in notebooks. A suicide note. He believed it was the end times. But we have that…we have your friend in the hallway having some kind of drug-induced psychotic break, and now this perfectly healthy lady who sat and starved to death in her apartment full of food."

"She starved?" Donna asked. Her voice felt foreign, like it was coming from someone she didn't recognize.

"They've already pretty much decided she died of malnutrition," he noted. "She had no body fat to speak of. You saw her. She didn't even leave any dead person goo on the chair."

Donna couldn't control the way her hands shook.

"That's impossible. She had been eating so much. She'd been doing great with her new diet and everything… Well, I say that, but she had eaten so much. There was garbage everywhere. It was like she just started binging and eating everything in sight. So she'd had food. Before I found her body, I had started cleaning."

"Why were you cleaning her apartment?"

"That's what I do. Before the pandemic, I cleaned houses, businesses. Now I just clean the apartments on this floor."

"That must have really put you in a financial bind."

"It has."

"So you must really know the people that live here. Probably better than anyone else."

Donna nodded slowly. It was the same logic that Mahlon had used when he needed someone to get everyone to take Limos. Someone who knew everyone's flaws and deepest desires, the thing that made them desperate for a quick fix. Someone they all trusted.

"Do you know of anything that the two people from your floor may have had in common?"

"Linda and Conrad? No. They couldn't have been more different as people. Linda was very—"

She paused. She wasn't sure if she should say anything negative about either person. Did she need a lawyer? Was she incriminating herself? She took a deep breath through her nose, reminding herself that she only knew them as neighbors and because she cleaned their apartments.

And the pills. She couldn't rule it out, not yet.

"You can be frank. We don't suspect any kind of foul play. We are more concerned about some kind of mold or fungus in the air systems, contaminants in the water, residual effects of the virus, a new street drug. We have no idea, but we want to cover all of our bases."

"Linda didn't associate with the rest of us much, unless it was to remind us that she was better than her neighbors. It was all a ruse, though. Conrad never bothered anyone. He was always nice, pleasant. If you needed anything, he would do whatever you needed him to."

"Do you know if Conrad was doing any kind of drugs or anything?"

"We had heard rumors but never saw any proof of it," Donna admitted, but then she had recalled how he had snorted the contents of the Limos capsule without hesitation. "Like I said, he was always very pleasant. Did an autopsy show what drug he was on that made him…do that?"

"Unfortunately, not yet. There are so many new drugs

on the streets every day, though, we may never get a straight answer from toxicology. We're doing the best we can with what resources we have, especially with the current state of things. We're shorthanded, labs are shorthanded, transportation is shit. But yeah, yeah, we think he was definitely on some kind of intense illegal drug. Maybe a synthetic psychedelic."

Donna didn't respond, instead looking down to pick at her fingernails to let him know she had nothing else to say about Conrad.

"When was the last time you spoke to or saw Linda?"

"I don't remember for sure. Maybe the day before yesterday? I'm sorry, for some reason my time is just really running together."

The detective's eyebrows furrowed, and a look of what was very convincing concern took over his features. He shifted in his seat. Maybe it wasn't a concern for her, though; maybe it was a concern that she may have some guilt on her mind. Maybe she *was* a suspect.

"Is everything okay?"

"Yes, I think so. Just been very busy."

"Well, you know what they say: the more time you have, the more time you need. Greedy son of a bitch."

"I do have a question," Donna added, hesitant. The detective nodded at her, motioning with his hand for her to continue. Her voice was unsure as she went on, although she tried to sound both curious and confident. "It may be nothing, but it does also seem strange to me that she was in such a state so quickly. Last I saw her she looked fine. Seemed to feel fine. In fact, she told me it was the best she had felt since she was a teenager."

"Did that seem odd?"

"Odd how?"

"Just odd in any way."

"No, I don't think so. I think the condition of her body was odd, though, don't you? She looked mummified or something."

"That I do not know. I'll leave it to the creeps in the lab to decide." The detective stood up, handing her a card with his name on it. He picked the notebook up off of the table and shut the cover with a satisfying pop before tucking it under his arm and putting his pen into his pocket. Donna watched as the still-open pen left a bleeding stain of ink on his white shirt.

He spoke again, jarring her out of her observation: "Just in case you think of anything else, here's my card. Feel free to call if you think of anything at all, or if you have any concerns about the other tenants. *Anything.*"

"Absolutely, detective. Thank you so much."

Donna took the card and left Linda's apartment for the last time. She tucked the card into her pocket and found that there was a matching card from this detective already resting there, a little more frayed and less pristine. She'd forgotten about meeting the handsome detective the day before and that he had already given her one of his cards.

Donna couldn't help but wonder what else she was forgetting.

DAY FOUR

Donna scrubbed the floor of Conrad's old apartment with a hard-bristled brush. It was as though she snapped out of some kind of trance mid-swipe, and she paused, panting with the broom handle clutched in her callused hands. The apartment seemed smaller instead of larger when it had been cleaned out and all of Conrad's things had been moved out. Now the apartment was up for rent again, and another person would move in and become a normal part of their lives. Everyone would forget Conrad, and it would be like he had never existed.

Maybe that was for the best. She didn't want to think about it that way, but the detective had said that it was very likely that Conrad had been taking some gnarly illicit substances and that had contributed to his mental break. She had to stop long enough to press her fingers into her eyes as she saw a flash of the fear she had seen on his face. It was burned into her brain like a white-hot light.

She tossed the floor brush out into the hallway and picked up her supply caddy before she headed out. She stopped in the doorway, looking over the empty room.

"Goodbye, Conrad," she whispered and shut the door.

It felt final this way, and the door felt like it sealed exceptionally tight.

Donna twisted the caps tight on the cleaning supplies, pausing in surprise at the girth of the soft plastic pencil case that she had stuffed in the back pocket of the caddy. It was bulging with cash. How much did she have now? She couldn't remember if she had counted it recently, but she knew this seemed like a lot more than she remembered. She'd make it a point to check it this evening when she was settled in from working. She chanted the mental note over and over in her head as she moved on to the next apartment.

She knocked on the door of Marian's apartment and heard the faint voice from inside that said: "Donna? Come on in."

Donna struggled with her brush, broom, and caddy and pushed the door open. Marian was Donna's favorite client because she was already *so clean*. It required so little that it was almost immoral for Donna to accept money for a full clean, but Marian always insisted she take the full amount. She entered the apartment and was immediately greeted by the scent of cinnamon and clove. Maybe a little pine. Was it close to Christmas? Was it winter outside? Christ. What was going on with her? She hadn't had this intense of a brain fog in years.

"Marian? I'm here to clean some. Where would you like me to start so that I'm out of your way?"

She heard Marian's voice again. "Actually, I'm in the bedroom. Can you please come help me?"

Donna set her things by the door and walked through the pristine living area to the bedroom. Marian was sitting up in her bed with the cover still pulled up around her arms, as though she had just sat up when Donna had knocked.

"Did I wake you? I'm sorry, I've been so out of it recently. I don't know what day it is or what time it is…"

"No, no. Quite all right. I am not feeling well, and I really need to get out of bed, but I'm having some trouble. Can you just give me a hand and help me onto my feet?"

Donna nodded slowly, approaching the bedside where she noted that Marian looked pale and drawn. She had a brief panic that maybe she was wasting away like Linda had. She quelled that fear as she came close enough to touch Marian, feeling her soft flesh around her bones. She was just tired. Who knew what she was going through? Donna should really keep up with her more.

She put her hand on Marian's elbow and stabilized her as Marian swung her legs over the edge and put her feet onto the floor.

"Oh my God, Marian. Are you—"

She couldn't help but gape at Marian's swollen belly as the woman ran her hands across it. The smile on her face was elated but also hysterical. It was the look of a woman who had snapped. Her brown eyes were so wide that they were rimmed on all sides by white. Her pupils were dilated with intense stimulation, and her smile was so broad that her cheeks twitched.

"Yes, isn't it wonderful? It's what I've always wanted," Marian said, batting her eyelashes at her. "I really have you to thank. The pill you gave us, it must have done it. I have been trying for years. *Years*, Donna, and all it took was just one pill."

"Just one pill…" Donna repeated weakly.

"Of course, I was afraid I couldn't maintain the pregnancy," Marian said as she hoisted herself onto her feet. Her stomach sagged halfway down her thighs. "Mahlon came to check on me, really nice man, and he offered me more. I took them just in case, but he said that one was all I needed. I just wanted to be sure. He cut me a good deal on them. I hope that didn't mess with any commission you might have gotten or anything… We've got nine months of this, so I'm happy to—"

"Marian, you shouldn't be this large… It's been…a day? Two days? I think you need a doctor. This isn't natural. This isn't right."

Marian's gaze turned venomous, and she glared at Donna, shoving her away. Donna stumbled backward in surprise. Marian's eyes were still as wide as an owl's, but now she was scowling with her teeth bared like an animal.

"I didn't mean anything bad," Donna whispered. "I'm

just worried about you. This isn't normal. You have to know this isn't normal."

"Well, if you can't be happy for us, I'm just going to need you to go." She stabbed her finger in the air toward the door, bob cut bouncing above her shoulders with the force of the motion.

"Marian, no—"

Donna was cut off when Marian suddenly doubled over, clutching at her stomach as she vomited onto the floor. The vomit was streaked with blood and smelled like actual shit. Donna put her hand across her mouth, trying to mask the fact that she was covering her nose to shield herself from the odor.

Marian groaned, all but roaring into the space between her and Donna. The sound reverberated not only in the room, but inside Donna's skull. The woman suddenly reared back, spine arching backward as she clawed at her shirt, pulling it up over her swollen abdomen to look down at it.

Donna screamed, stifling the unexpected sound with both hands.

Marian's stomach was not only enormous, but it was full of massive, bulbous growths. It looked like a fleshy sack of marbles, and it rippled against her flesh and pulsed. Veins pressed against the surface of her skin, which was pulled so thin that you could have pinched and lifted the vessels away without effort.

She stumbled toward Donna, reaching out to her as

she wailed. Donna backed away in horror, and if she hadn't been so terrified she would have fled. Marian tripped over the rug as she walked toward Donna again, falling face down onto the floor. The noise that resounded was like a gunshot or a popping balloon: a loud and sharp pop that startled Donna so much that she thought she may have pissed her pants just a little.

Marian rolled over to reveal that her stomach had burst down the middle like the split of a perfectly ripe watermelon. A stream of red fluid reminiscent of frog spawn poured from her abdomen: hundreds if not thousands of gelatinous bubbles with budding eye spots that gave them the appearance of seeds suspended in jelly. Marian reached down, wheezing as she grabbed armfuls of her to-be-babies and tried to scoop them back into her cavity.

Donna darted toward the door, slipping on the slickness of the floor and falling flat into the farthest reaches of the mess. Marian screamed at the sight of the crushed babies, but Donna didn't stop. Her shoes squeaked on the wet floor as she found her footing and rushed out of the apartment and down the hall.

She took the stairs more slowly, shoes still slick and wet. More than once she looked down and dusted off a piece of Marian's uterine contents off of herself. The security office loomed at the other end of the hall on the bottom floor, and that hall felt like it stretched on forever. Her head was swimming, and she felt like she was going to faint. She just needed to hang on long enough to talk to Ralph and either have him call the police or she would call the detective herself.

But what if he thought she had something to do with it? What if she *did* have something to do with it? If he could link her to the deaths of so many people, she'd most certainly be put in prison for the rest of her life.

The security office finally loomed to her right, door already open and inviting.

"Ralph?" Donna croaked, clearing her throat and calling his name again.

She entered the office, stopping short when she noticed Ralph's unmoving body in his chair.

Donna clutched the doorway, letting a scream of exasperation escape her lips as she looked at the mutated body of the security guard. He was huge: body bulging with muscles upon muscles. His flesh looked slick with sweat; veins in his neck and head had burst into purple and black flowers. His head was thrown back, bloody froth coming out of his mouth and nose. There were marks on his throat where he had clawed at it. She wondered if all of that muscle in his massive neck had collapsed his trachea. His shirt was open, and her shoe had landed on a stray button; when she looked down she saw them scattered everywhere.

Donna spun back away to keep from looking at him, clutching at the door, and then the wall as she inevitably descended onto the floor and everything went dark.

DAY FIVE

Donna awoke face down on the floor in the hallway outside of Ralph's office: exactly where she had fallen. Her entire body ached, wrist throbbing with pain where she had tried to stop herself from hitting her face on the floor. She struggled onto her knees, letting herself adjust from the pain of laying on the cold tile. She could lean back just an inch or so and see the knees of Ralph as he sat dead in his chair. She had to look, just until she saw his knees, to confirm that she had really seen him.

It was the Limos; it had to be.

Donna reached up to touch her face, then her neck, and then her chest. If it *was*, though, why did she not have some deformity like Linda, Marian, and Ralph? Why didn't she go insane like Conrad?

Oh, God, someone else had taken the Limos that day. Gertrude.

"No, no, no, no." Donna sobbed, limping to the staircase.

She would never forgive herself if something happened to Gertrude. She was her best friend, maybe the only friend she had in this godforsaken world. She struggled through the murky memories of the last few days to try and remember what it was that Gertrude had taken the Limos for. What was it that she needed it to do for her?

Donna all but dragged her body up each stair: she was in pain and her muscles felt like they were made of lead.

Marian's door was still standing wide open: a sign that no one had been in the hall since she had gone outside. There was no sound from inside, but that didn't keep Donna from shying away from the entrance as though the eviscerated mother might come charging out at her.

She leaned on Gertrude's door in paranoia and banged on it with her fists. Donna knew something was wrong. She knew that going into Gertrude's apartment was going to reveal something terrible had happened to the elderly woman. She couldn't ignore the feeling that settled over her: a grim acceptance, a premeditated grief.

"Gertrude? Jesus, please tell me you're in there." She didn't try to hide the horror in her voice as she screamed into the door.

When there was no response, she took her keys in her shaking hands and fumbled for Gertrude's, unlocking the door as soon as she located it and slipping inside. Everything was quiet. Her stacks of romance novels sat with dust on them, a cup of tea on the table had long since gone cold. Gertrude's glasses lay on the counter in the bathroom. This was the most sobering find so far. Gertrude couldn't see anything without her glasses.

Donna heard a sound from the bedroom. The hair raised along her spine as she crept towards the noise: a low sort of coo that she couldn't identify. Her ears rang as she strained to hear the distant sound again. Gertrude's bedroom was likewise unoccupied. The bed was tousled and at first glance appeared to be empty, and then she saw the sheets stir. Just enough of a shift that she barely noticed it. Donna's brow furrowed in confusion as the sheets jerked again.

She stepped toward it, taking a deep breath before she pulled the sheets back to discover a baby laying in the middle of Gertrude's nightgown. At the sight of her, it made another excited coo and then blew a raspberry between its lips.

"Gertrude?" she breathed.

Youth. Gertrude had wanted to be young again, and here she was an infant. Donna reached for the baby with shaking hands, and then something rushed into her head. It was like a window opened and sucked the breath out of the room and her lungs all at the same time. That same sensation of cold water being dumped overhead hit her again as realization struck her.

She had a baby.

"Jacob."

When was the last time that she had seen her child? Who had been taking care of him? She couldn't remember anything from the last several days other than cleaning and all of the bizarre deaths. She didn't remember anything at all; she hadn't cared about anything, worried about anything. It was a blur. How could she have forgotten her own baby?

Donna sprinted to her apartment, ignoring the smell that harassed her senses the moment she entered. She knew from the silence, from the odor of death, that

Jacob was gone. She tore the apartment apart looking for him, but he was nowhere to be found. Her own apartment was uncleaned and looked so neglected. Had she even slept this week? Her head throbbed with stress.

"Jakey, honey," she called, checking the bathroom and behind all of the furniture.

Eventually she found a dark place on the floor: just a mass of black and brown next to a dirty, overfilled diaper. The mass pulsed with the rhythm of maggots as they stirred within what she knew in her heart was the decayed corpse of her baby.

Donna was overwhelmed with anger; the fury saved her from the hammer of sorrow that threatened to come down and crush her soul. She stormed out of her apartment and down the hall, heading straight for Mahlon's room. To her surprise, the door opened upon her approach, as though it had expected her.

Mahlon stood behind his desk with his hands crossed. She would have cleared the desk and tackled him to the floor, but she felt the forward propulsion of her body stop when he raised his hand to her.

"Sit, Donna."

And she did. She didn't want to, and she didn't make the decision to sit, but she sat.

"I want to thank you for distributing Limos for me here. You did such a good job." He smiled. "I'm happy to report that this soft launch is an overwhelming success.

One hundred percent success rate, actually, so we're ready to go worldwide."

"A success?" Donna felt tears pour from her eyes. "How was this a success? Everyone is dead and it's your fault, isn't it? It was the Limos?"

Mahlon smiled at her like a parent smiled at a child who couldn't understand a complex concept. He sat down, sliding the scale back to the center of the table. He pointed at it again with a long finger.

"Limos gives the consumer whatever it is they desire and however intensely they desire it. I never make anyone take anything. I use the power of suggestion, the illusion of the almighty free will. Mankind is addicted to this sort of thing; they make it *so easy*. Offer them an easy way to get these trivial, meaningless things and they'll take it no questions asked. No one ever wants happiness, health… No. They want to be thin, they want to be buff, they want to be young… I'll admit that I didn't know how Conrad's situation would fare, but let's just say it was clear that he wasn't ready to see what he thought he sought. Give people the opportunity to indulge, to have excess… They'll choose famine for a taste of debauchery *every time*."

She wanted to ask him who he really was, *what* he really was. She wanted to ask him why he was doing this and why he had chosen this place, but another question seemed more important to ask.

"And what about me? I didn't ask for this. Jacob was

my everything. I didn't ask to be skinny or strong or any of those things. I would never trade my child for anything. I would never have agreed to this if I had known…"

"What's that saying… Hindsight is twenty-twenty? Do you remember what you told me you wanted when I offered you the Limos and weighed your soul on the scales?"

Donna shook her head, eyes so brimmed with tears that Mahlon was rippling in her blurred vision. She hadn't asked him for anything, had she?

"What was it? Time?" Mahlon cooed.

"Yes," Donna whispered. "I asked for more time."

"Now that he's gone, you have all the time in the world, don't you?"

Donna closed her eyes, teeth set so tightly that her jaw squeaked. When she opened them, Mahlon was gone. The room was empty but had such a heaviness that she nearly sank to the floor with the weight of it. She could hear the sound of Gertrude wailing from her apartment, but she knew that soon she would disappear: de-aging to the point that she was microscopic cells on the sheets of her bed. And for Donna time would stretch on and on…

She took a deep breath, leaning forward to put her hands on the table to stand.

She noticed the scale on the table was even and balanced, and on the right plate sat one black pill.

Death (Pale Horse)

When the Lamb broke the fourth seal, I heard the voice of the fourth living creature saying, "Come". I looked, and behold, an ashen horse; and he who sat on it had the name Death; and Hades was following with him. Authority was given to them over a fourth of the Earth, to kill with sword and with famine and with pestilence and by the wild beasts of the Earth.

—Revelation 6:7−8

FADE TO BLACK

R.E. SARGENT

CHAPTER ONE

The shadows in the room dissipated as the screen flickered, a result of the dark and light contrast of the video that was playing. The lights were off, and Troy preferred to work that way. His fingers danced over the keyboard. Although he didn't type conventionally with his fingers in the right positions, he typed quickly and efficiently, the result of years of mastering his craft. The video actually only played out on one of the four screens that were displayed in front of him: Metal music that inspired him… Videos that kept him entertained.

He reread the code that he had just perfected—a year and a half in the creation stage, but it wasn't until this night that he figured out the broken code that was keeping things from working the way he had envisioned.

A sickly smile etched itself across his face as he contemplated the repercussions of his next actions. What the hell was wrong with him? Where had his moral compass gone?

The answer was he didn't have one… He never had. It wasn't his parents' fault, but he had always been drawn to the macabre. His fantasies had involved hurting people, not helping them.

At twenty-three years old, Troy was anything but ordinary. Not by his intelligence. Not by his actions. And certainly not by his appearance. His greasy hair almost resembled a bowl cut… not by choice or design, but because he chose to go to the shitty chain haircutting place in the strip mall down the street from his house. Every cut was the same price and every cut was just as shitty as the next one. Troy didn't care. He had other things to spend his money on.

Like the fifteen-thousand-dollar computer setup he had in front of him.

He was tall and wiry, and as much as he snacked, it was odd how he stayed so skinny. Sickly skinny. Like all arms and legs connected to a beanpole torso. He resembled a praying mantis, although his skin was pasty white instead of green. His neck was too long, which made his gangly appearance even more pronounced.

Troy resolved himself to the fact that he would never have a girlfriend. That realization came to be imprinted in his mind early on when he tried to ask the pretty girls—and some not-so-pretty girls—from his classes out on dates in both junior high and high school. He had been rejected each and every time, and eventually, he decided it was time to stop humiliating himself. Instead, he found extreme satisfaction from hardcore masturbation. Anytime he thought about dating, he would run off a batch and the thought would leave his mind. But Troy didn't watch porn; he wasn't an ordinary masturbator. He fantasized about blood, gore, death, and decay. That's what got Troy off. His dick got hard watching other people die.

The most crushing part of Troy's existence wasn't the fact that he couldn't get laid. It wasn't even the fact that he had no friends. And it didn't bother him that his fetishes were not normal. To him they were. What bothered him was he had never really truly seen anybody die. The deaths were all either acted out, or suspect internet deaths that could easily have been staged. Hell, now that AI was becoming prevalent in everyday life, he wondered how many of those dark web deaths were simply the result of a talented AI program.

Troy got up from his desk and went to the kitchen. He pulled some pizza rolls out of the freezer, slid a plate out of the cabinet, and arranged twenty pockets on the plate. Always twenty, never nineteen or twenty-one. He set the microwave for the correct amount of time, and after putting the pizza pockets inside, he started it. In the fridge, he grabbed a Coke and popped the top. As he waited for the microwave, he looked around. He took in the clutter and the dirt and realized that eventually he was going to have to get his ass in gear and clean. He didn't like living like this, but he spent long hours coding at his keyboard, and something had to give. What gave was mostly sleep and picking up after himself.

Although he didn't have anyone to answer to, and he lived alone, when things got really out of place, it messed with his OCD and his anxiety.

As the timer went off on the microwave, he could feel the anxiety creeping in, and he went to his bathroom and grabbed a couple Hydroxyzine, popping them in his mouth and dry-swallowing them.

Back in the kitchen, Troy grabbed his pizza pockets and his Coke and went back to his keyboard. He stared at the screen for a moment, knowing all he had to do was push the fucking button. He smiled to himself, an internal pat on his own back. Then he clicked the mouse and initiated the upload.

Troy sat and ate while he watched the process on the screen as the coding was uploaded.

He took a moment and reached deep down inside himself to make sure that he was not going to regret what he was about to do. He couldn't put the toothpaste back in the tube on this one. Once he unleashed the fuckery, there was no unfucking it. And as for Troy, he would be famous… infamous even. What would become of him, he did not know. And if he were to be honest with himself, he didn't care. The world would know Troy's name, and that was all that mattered.

CHAPTER TWO

Marnie Fischer finished packing up the ice chests in the kitchen. Her husband Robb walked in just as she closed the lid on the second chest.

"Perfect timing!" she said. "Did you want to help me carry these out to the garage?"

"Sure, honey. I just finished loading all of the other gear into the truck. Is all of the food packed?"

"Yes. We just need to stop on our way out of town and get ice."

"Works for me. We need to gas up the Dodge anyway."

"How long of a drive is it to the spot that Joe and Emily found?" Marnie asked.

"I think Joe said it was about three hours. I can't wait

to check it out though… He said it is secluded as fuck, but there are natural springs coming out the side of the mountain. He showed me a few pictures. It looks phenomenal."

"Do you think it will be crowded?"

"Honestly, Marnie, I don't even know if anyone knows about this place. Joe stumbled on it by accident, and there weren't any signs of other people staying there."

"So are we meeting them there? How will we find it?"

"No," Robb said. "They are meeting us in the little town down at the base of the mountain. We will follow them up in their Expedition."

"Oh, they are bringing the Expedition? Why the fuck aren't we all just riding up in that? It's so roomy."

"They have a lot of gear as well. I don't think we could all fit in there with all of our gear. Besides, it's always good to have a second vehicle in case one breaks down."

"Don't jinx it, babe!" Marnie laughed.

Robb carried the ice chests out to the truck and loaded them in the second row of the cab. Marnie walked around the house and looked to make sure they hadn't forgotten anything. Simultaneously, Robb glanced through every-thing in the garage and shed, making sure that nothing was left behind.

"Ready to go, babe?" Robb called from the driveway.

"I'll be right out," Marnie said. She ran into the bathroom and relieved herself before the long trip. She thought about how nice it was going to be to get away for a four-day weekend with Joe and Emily. The four of them were best friends and had been for years. It always seemed like there was never enough time to get together and someone was always too busy, but for some reason when Marnie had suggested this trip, Joe and Emily jumped on it, and Robb was on board as well. She decided she would have to be more persistent in the future. Life was too damn short to work your ass off week after week and not take time to play. They would definitely try to make up for it this weekend.

After making sure all the doors were locked, Marnie exited through the garage, and as she climbed into the lifted truck, Robb clicked the button to roll the overhead door down.

"Ready, babe?" he asked.

"So damn ready."

Robb started the truck and glanced over at the neighbor's house. True to form, the elderly lady was standing at the window. Robb waved. Marnie noticed who he was waving at and waved also as the neighbor returned the wave.

"She's so sweet," Marnie said.

"Yeah, she is. But she's always at that damned window," Robb said, chuckling.

"She's just lonely, babe. We are the closest thing to a

family she has, which is so sad. I can't understand why her children don't come around."

"Probably a bunch of ungrateful assholes," Robb said.

"Probably."

Robb pulled out of the driveway and onto their street. At the stop sign on the corner, he turned right, driving toward the main street that ran through town. They would stop at the convenience store at the edge of town and top off the tank, grabbing the ice while they were there.

"When's the last time we did something like this?" Robb asked.

"Forever ago. Maybe a couple of years?"

"Seems like it. I'm glad we are doing it."

"Me too. Can't think of anything better right now. I just hope the spot is as good as everyone is pumping it up to be."

Robb smiled. "From the pictures Joe showed me, it's looking pretty promising."

"Good. Hopefully I can work on my tan."

Robb laughed.

"What's so funny?" she asked.

Robb looked over at Marnie and ran his eyes over her. She was a small girl, not just in height, but she was also thin. Although she would never divulge her weight, Robb figured she couldn't be much more than one hundred pounds. She wore a blue bikini top, cleavage spilling out, and a pair of denim cut-off shorts over her bikini bottoms. A jeweled piece of jewelry hung down from her belly button. Her long, blond hair touched her lap.

"What's funny is you are already tan AF," he said.

"Not even close," she said, scoffing. "But I'm glad you think so."

Robb took one last look, took a deep breath, and turned his attention back to the road. He knew he had definitely lucked out ending up with Marnie. Although they had gone to high school together, they knew each other but were never close. Robb's shyness had kept him from dating much in high school, but he had always thought Marnie to be a stunner.

After graduation, it was years later, when they were in their late twenties, that they ran into each other again. Robb and Joe, who had worked together at one of the local grocery stores and became good friends, had attended a Metallica concert one mild summer day. It was while they were working their way toward the stage that Robb spotted her. Marnie was just as stunning as he remembered her to be, all those years later. He did a double-take when he saw her and immediately felt the crushing shyness take charge, even though he had worked so hard over the years to work through it and be social. Marnie immediately brought that little high-school shy boy back from the dead. As quickly as he was about to say something to her, he turned away and headed toward the stage.

It was her hand on his arm that had stopped him.

"Robb? Is that really fucking you?" she had asked.

She remembered him. And it was that night that he had found out that she had always thought he was a cutie but figured he wasn't interested since he never talked to her.

And it was also that night that Marnie's friend, Emily, became smitten with Robb's friend, Joe. They all hung out that night at the concert, followed it up by having breakfast around midnight at the local Dennys, and finally parting ways with each other's company around three a.m. Later that day, they were all together again. And the next day.

Robb and Marnie quickly fell head over heels with each other, and within a year, they were married and bought a house. Joe and Emily had a similar story, although they hadn't gotten married. That didn't stop them from moving in together.

Robb glanced over again and took in her tan, swollen breasts, feeling like he was getting away with something. Marnie caught him looking.

"What are you looking at?"

"Nothing."

"Were you staring at my tits?"

"I think they were staring at me."

"Yeah, that's probably it," she said, laughing.

"Can't wait to get our tent up and our air mattress set up. Maybe we can take a *nap*." He added extra emphasis on the word nap.

"Slow down, dude. You have all weekend to plow this field. Let's not immediately disappear and leave Joe and Emily to their own devices. You have to wait until tonight."

"Party pooper."

"Don't worry. I'll make it up to you."

"You better."

Robb turned into the store parking lot and, after finding an open dispenser, pumped the gas while Marnie went inside to pay for the ice. When she came back out, Robb helped her grab the ice from the merchandiser outside the store. He slammed it on the concrete to break it up and handed the bags to Marnie, who dumped them into the ice chests.

Back in the truck, they talked about the upcoming weekend excitedly as they drove. The hour to the nearby town went by quickly, and Robb turned into the agreed-upon parking lot and looked for Joe's Expedition. Marnie spotted it at the far end of the lot, and Robb navigated through the parking aisles until they pulled in beside them.

Joe and Emily hopped out of the Expedition, and Robb and Marnie climbed out of the truck as well. Robb shook Joe's hand and then pulled him in for a man hug. Joe was a tad taller at about six foot, two inches, while Robb was right around six foot. Both were of a medium build, but Robb was clean shaven and Joe had a beard that he had been growing for the past year.

Marnie ran to Emily, who was six inches taller than Marnie and just as attractive with fiery red hair and green eyes. She threw her in a tight hug and then went over and hugged Joe, while Robb took his turn hugging Emily.

"Are you guys ready for this?" Joe asked.

"Sooo ready," Marnie answered.

"Been looking forward to it all week," Robb added.

"It's gonna be awesome," Emily said.

"How long of a drive is it?" Marnie asked.

"A couple hours," Joe said.

"Do you guys want to grab a bite before we head up the mountain?" Robb asked.

Joe and Emily looked at each other and nodded.

"Let's do it!" Joe said. "Where?"

"How about that Chipotle down the street?" Marnie said.

"That sounds fantastic, Marnie," Robb said. "Does that work for you guys?" he asked Joe and Emily.

"Perfect," Joe answered, and Emily nodded.

CHAPTER THREE

Rosemary Taylor stood at the window, watching as the young couple next door climbed into their truck. She caught the young male's attention and waved, and her reward was receiving a wave back from both of them. She smiled at them as they pulled out of the driveway.

Her kitchen window overlooked the front of their

house, and she always found herself drawn to it. She had a problem with being a little nosey, and she fully admitted it, but she tried not to be too intrusive.

The kids that lived there, Robb and Marnie, were so sweet to her. They even invited her over to dinner occasionally. She never turned down their offer.

The neighborhood was sparse with only ten or so houses, and she didn't know most of the neighbors. The ones on the other side of her were assholes, so she avoided them. Across the street was nothing but a big field that the owners used to plant pumpkins and who knew what else. But she had lucked out when the younger couple moved in. She had no one in life, so she got in her social time by chatting with them, eating a meal with them, crocheting them blankies and other goodies, and other interactions. Truth be told, she was quite fond of them.

Marnie told her they were going out of town for a long weekend, but she had forgotten. The packing of the truck had caught her off guard for a moment, but then she remembered. They both worked so much, she was happy to see that they were getting away for some much needed rest, but she was also sad. Sad that she would be alone for several days.

After the truck disappeared down the road, Rosemary sighed. When she wasn't cooking or cleaning, her activities were fairly limited. She either read a good book or crocheted something for someone. A year earlier, Robb had set her up with a bunch of television channels, and she had learned what binge-watching was all about. This weekend would be all about binge-watching a show that she had wanted to see for a long time but had never started. Unless the neighborhood squirrels put on a show, the window would hold no action over the next few days as the only view she had was the neighbor's property and nothing else.

She filled her iced tea glass, grabbed a few Lifesavers out of the candy dish, grabbed the remote from the small table by her recliner, and settled in, using the motorized footrest to prop up her feet. She pressed play, and the screen came to life.

CHAPTER FOUR

Troy watched the phone as it continued to ring. The caller ID announced the caller as THEM. The name he had collectively given his parents. The phone fell silent finally, but Troy knew that in a few minutes, when the voicemail cut his mother off after several minutes of her incessant rambling, the fragmented voicemail would announce itself in his inbox. And the rhetoric would be the same. *Why don't you ever return our calls? We're worried sick over you. Are you getting enough to eat? Do you want to go with us to church on Sunday?*

The answer to that last question was, and always would be, a big fucking no. Growing up, he had been forced to go to church with them Sunday morning and Sunday evening, as well as Wednesday night. Their religion was shoved down his throat. But their religion wasn't his. In fact, he wasn't religious in any form. Instead, he felt in his element when surrounded by the darkness. The macabre.

His parents weren't terrible. They did the best they could. Troy simply didn't connect with them. Really had no common interests with them. He'd much rather be alone in his small apartment than be with them. And it was easier to ignore them than answer their tiring questions. Besides, if they knew what he was up to, they would certainly try to stop him. It was better if they kept their distance. Better for everyone.

Troy looked down at the front of his gray sweats. The translucent pearl-colored fluid puddled in the front, which had formed a type of bowl shape after he had slipped them down around his thighs.

He had almost been cock-blocked by his own mother when her call came through right as he was about to shoot his glorious bounty, four different videos of destruction playing across the four different monitors. He had felt himself pulled away from orgasm but had somehow double downed on his stroking speed and took himself over the edge, forgetting to grab the wad of tissues setting on the edge of the desk to catch the mess in the process.

He had basically spewed all over himself while his

mother was leaving him a voicemail asking what he was doing.

Beating my meat, Mom. What else?

He wiped the stickiness from his shaft and winced when he scraped the tissues over tender flesh. His stroking speed had burned a patch of flesh off his member, and it pulled him out of the ecstasy he had been under.

In the bathroom, he ran the water until it got warm, soaked a washcloth, and cleaned the tender flesh, making sure to get all the cum off.

Deciding there were parts dirtier than his junk, he stripped out of his jism-covered clothes, hopped in the shower, and vigorously scrubbed his entire body. He laughed out loud at the irony. No matter how clean his body was, he would always be dirty: his actions, his mind, his soul. He knew where he would end up when this life was over, and he embraced it.

When he toweled off and put on some clean clothes, he put in a DoorDash order for some food. He was famished.

His food showed up half an hour later and he scarfed it down. A tomato turkey sub sandwich, kettle chips, potato salad, and a brownie. A meal that left him over full, but in a happy mood.

Feeling too stuffed to sit at his desk, he laid down on the couch to watch a little television. Using the voice remote, he brought up the movie *2012*, one of the movies he liked to watch a few times a year just for the body count alone.

He watched every minute with a smile on his face. Inside, his guts felt giddy and euphoric. When the credits rolled, he felt satiated. And without realizing it, his eyelids grew heavy and closed, his breathing increasingly deeper and breathy.

CHAPTER FIVE

Chelle set the plastic bowl of macaroni and cheese in front of her five-year-old daughter, Kayla. Always a good little eater, Kayla spooned the noodles into her mouth as she watched her favorite show on the television in the dining area. While Chelle certainly didn't feel like mother of the year for using the television to keep Kayla in line, especially during mealtime, she was doing the best she could. Getting out of bed in the morning was hard enough for her… Taking care of her daughter took all of her energy.

She hadn't always felt the grip of depression clamping down on her throat. It was when she had received the news about Michael that had destroyed her world and her lust for life. It was hard enough for her while he was deployed. And Kayla suffered the most, only seeing her dad over FaceTime and only when he could get an internet connection. Kayla had only seen him twice in person before he got himself blown up. And now Kayla's daily questions about why Daddy wasn't calling on the phone dwindled to every other day, then a couple times a week, and now rarely. Chelle hadn't had the heart to tell their daughter that Daddy was dead, and now she was regretting that decision exponentially.

She watched as Kayla finished her lunch, knowing that she would have a couple hours to herself when Kayla took her nap. Hours she desperately needed to distract herself from the life that she was not living, but merely sludging through. A life without the man of her dreams. And a shit-load of guilt for Kayla not being enough for her to move past it. Even though she loved Kayla with all her heart and being, the sweet child could not erase Chelle's pain. She knew she was failing the little girl, yet she couldn't seem to pull herself out of her funk even after almost two years.

After lunch, with Kayla tucked safely in bed, Chelle pulled out her phone and started scrolling through social media, getting lost in the memes and videos. The world outside disappeared as Chelle sunk into an online world that would forever be her distraction.

That was the first time she saw the video. An announcement of sorts of some event that she was assured she couldn't miss. An event that was shrouded in mystery. A poster that she didn't know, yet the algorithms had magically thrown the video into her feed. The thought of the unknown was exciting. *I can't just not attend. The FOMO would kill me.*

Her finger hovered over the event response button for a few seconds, and with a sudden burst of resolve, she pressed the "Interested" button.

CHAPTER SIX

Joe finished off his burrito bowl and looked up to catch Marnie smiling at him.

"What?" he asked, self-consciously.

"Nothing," she said, smirking. "Just admiring how you tore into that bowl and left nothing behind."

"You know me… I don't like to waste food." His lips curled up at the corner, and his eyes scrunched up.

"Or," she said, "you just really like to eat."

"Don't judge me."

"No judgment here. At least you wear it well!"

"Why thank you," Joe said, his face slightly flushed.

"Are you flirting with my man, Marnie?" Emily asked playfully.

"Oh of course. Hitting on him right here in the local Chipotle, with his wife sitting right next to me. It's how I roll."

Emily elbowed Marnie in the ribs, and Marnie spit out her drink, resulting in everyone at the table breaking out in laughter.

When they had finished their meal, they made their way out to the vehicles.

"You following me, Robb?" Joe asked.

Robb decided to not be a smartass even though he knew no other way to get to their secret destination besides following.

"Yup! Let's go!"

They each hopped in their respective vehicles and left the parking lot, the Expedition leading the way. After half an hour, Joe pulled off the blacktop onto a dirt road that Robb hadn't even noticed was there.

The road was more of a trail, really: rocky, narrow, and overgrown by weeds.

"Wow, how did they ever discover this place?" Marnie asked.

"I was wondering the same thing. But Joe likes to explore. I'm guessing he found it randomly. I hope it's everything he's made it out to be."

"Has Emily been?"

"I think she said she went once. She had good things to say about it."

"I can't wait to get there."

"Same."

They rode the rest of the way in silence with the last half hour of the ride resulting in them climbing several steep hills. At a couple of points in the journey, when Marnie was simply positive the truck was going to flip over backward and roll down the steep incline, she grabbed the *Oh Shit* bar and white-knuckled it until they reached the top.

They had just breached one of the hilltops when Marnie let out a huge breath.

"That was fucking insane!"

"Right?" Robb said. "Brings back memories from my teenage years."

"You've done this stuff before?"

"Oh, all the time. In high school, I had a really nice lifted Toyota 4X4. People liked to hang with me simply because of that truck, and it got us to many remote party places. But we also liked to go find crazy four-wheel-drive trails and go a little wild. We had a couple hills like these back then, and the first time I tried to make it, I slid backward down the hill. It was terrifying, and I thought for sure I was gonna roll. The first lesson I learned is hit it hard, hit it fast, and never stop until you are on solid ground."

"Well, I guess I should be happy you have experience in this, otherwise I'd really be freaking out."

"I mean, you're freaking out a *little* bit," Robb said, laughing.

"Shut up and just get us there," she joked.

They continued following Joe, and Robb wondered how Joe remembered how to find the place with all of the different offshoots from the trail.

"How does he even remember how to get here?" Marnie asked.

Robb laughed. "I was just wondering the same exact thing."

The ground flattened out, and they wound their way back around a tree line. About fifteen minutes later, they drove around a small hill, and Joe pulled the Expedition up next to a tree and got out.

Robb pulled the truck up beside Joe and Emily's vehicle, shut it off, and he and Marnie opened the doors and got out.

The sound of the spring caught their attention, and their heads immediately turned to view the crystal-clear water flowing from a crack in the rocks. A small body of water pooled at the base, and the overflow spilled out and followed a small creek bed.

Taking in her surroundings, Marnie noticed a flat, grassy area under a huge tree, plenty of room to set up camp. There was a firepit approximately twenty feet away that she envisioned sitting around at night, the marshmallow sticks hovering over the flames, the marshmallows themselves turning a golden brown, waiting to join the chocolate in the graham cracker goodness. The spring was actually flowing out of a hill that rose up on one side of them, a backdrop that felt comforting and safe.

Robb let out a low whistle.

"Damn, dudes…this place is the shit."

"Right?" Joe said.

"And you found this place by accident?" Marnie asked.

"Yup. And I'm sure you saw all of the different splits

in the road. I've been on most of them. But this is the only place I've found up here that's as perfect as this one."

"It is pretty perfect," Emily agreed.

"Did you build the fire pit?" Marnie asked.

"Yes," Joe said. "We really haven't ever seen evidence of anyone else ever being here."

"And that little pool?" Robb said. "Couldn't be more perfect."

"Joe actually helped Mother Nature with that one," Emily said. "Brought a shovel up here one time and dug the hole out to the size it is now, then dumped a bunch of bags of pea gravel he hauled up here inside to line the bottom. It's not deep. How deep would you say it is, Joe?"

"Probably only like a few feet. Great to actually set a lawn chair in and hang out and stay cool. I think it's probably wide enough to accommodate all of us."

Marnie jumped up and down a little bit, and everyone laughed.

"Sorry! I'm just excited. Thanks for bringing us, guys!" she said to Joe and Emily.

"Glad we could all go do something together again," Joe said. "It's been a long time."

"Way too long," Marnie agreed.

"And we can't think of anyone we'd rather share this place with," Emily said. "Just promise you won't tell anyone about it. While Joe and I don't own it, it kind of feels like ours."

"Bet!" Robb said. "Your secret is safe with us."

Marnie pulled out her phone and looked at it.

"It's almost two o'clock."

"Yeah…we should get camp set up," Robb said.

"Oh crap. No cell service here," Marnie said.

"And you won't find it anywhere out here," Emily confirmed. "I've tried to walk around and even climbed to the top of the hill," she said, pointing. "Nothing. So put the phone away for the weekend and enjoy life a little."

"I'm not mad," Marnie said, smiling. "Looking forward to shutting out the outside world."

"Same," Robb said.

Marnie slid her phone back in her pocket, and the four of them began unloading the vehicles as they excitedly decided how to set up camp. The next few hours flew by, but they never noticed.

CHAPTER SEVEN

Troy stared at his monitors, his right pointer finger hovering over the enter button. It was time. He would spread the word. He choked down bile as his stomach betrayed him. He had checked the math at least a hundred times. If he was right, his message would reach farther than his limited imagination could comprehend.

Troy pressed enter. A rush of air left his lungs. He

knew there would be no visible results, yet he was disappointed that nothing went boom or that the world didn't fold in on itself. Still, he was anxious to check the results… to monitor them.

The video played in his online feed. He knew it well. He had written it, developed it, produced it. Taunting. Provoking. An invitation whose goal was to get people to join his broadcast on Sunday. A day many people would be at home next to their social media.

He pulled up the statistics. Zero views.

"FUCK!"

Had he screwed up? Did the video miss the mark? Would he have to start over? He had invested years in his process. Years!

He refreshed the screen and yelled when the information reloaded. Over two thousand views in a matter of minutes. Three hundred and forty-seven people interested in attending. When he refreshed again several minutes later, the numbers had almost doubled.

This is really happening.

The refresh button became his new obsession as he tapped it over and over, counting out loud in between presses, trying to hold out longer each time, yet like his masturbation addiction, he had little willpower and could not resist the urge to refresh over and over. Each update showed thousands more interested people. He was going viral.

He felt discomfort in his abdomen and realized he had

to pee badly, something he hadn't been paying attention to until his bladder screamed at him to take care of business. He unplugged the power cord from his laptop and carried it into the bathroom, sitting down on the toilet like a girl might, because he couldn't bear to be apart from his laptop for even a minute.

With his laptop sitting on his legs, the heat from the bottom slightly burning his skin, he continued to check his stats. His video was getting views from every country. Although he had hoped this would be the case, nagging doubt crept in often; was he just a poser? He would never be able to pull off such a grand feat. It would never work.

Yet here it was, the first half of his plan working. The goal here was to get as many viewers as possible to join his presentation the following night. He had something to show them. Something that would change their lives forever.

CHAPTER EIGHT

Rosemary woke up later than normal on Saturday morning. She could tell by the way the light was filtering through the window that it was late morning. An unheard of time for her to be climbing out of bed. The binge-watching of an entire season of shows on Netflix had taken its toll. Ten hours. She hadn't stayed up that late in years. She got a slow start to her day by puttering around, doing little besides straightening up a few things. Finally, she sat down with a hot cup of coffee and a bowl of shredded wheat. She couldn't be bothered to cook that morning, her energy tank on empty.

After washing her bowl and spoon and putting them in the dish drainer, she picked up the book she had been reading and settled into her chair. The faux leather felt soft on her skin, and she felt relaxed. Two chapters in, she felt herself struggling to stay awake and repeatedly pulled herself back to the book, rereading the same paragraph multiple times as she tried to remember what she had already read.

Finally, after struggling for thirty minutes, she slipped her bookmark into the book and shut it, setting it on the TV tray she had set up next to the chair. She slipped into a sound sleep immediately, her late night and age catching up to her. As a woman in her seventies, she found herself taking naps on an almost daily basis.

The barking from across the street woke her up, and she glanced at the clock. Two fifteen p.m. Must be the mailman. The dog across the street never failed to announce him, and then Rosemary heard the distinct snap of the mailbox lid being flipped closed. She then heard the engine as the Jeep accelerated toward the next house down the street.

She slipped her feet into her slippers and went out the front door. Her mailbox shared a post with the neighbors, so she gathered their mail as well as she many times did when they were away. She'd give the pile to them when they returned.

Back inside her house, she laid their mail in a pile on a little table by the door. She looked through the few things that came for her. An advertisement, her new auto insurance card, some other junk mail. Her hopes were high every time she went to the mailbox that there would be something good. A card or letter. A check. Anything really that could give her something to be excited about.

Sadly, she knew her life was boring and uneventful. She simply tolerated the monotony of each one of her final days on Earth, because that's the only choice she had. She only had the simple things to concentrate on. A half hour of laughter watching *Golden Girls*. A book that took her to another time and place. An interaction with the neighbors.

Rosemary adored Marnie, who reminded her of herself when she was younger. And she could tell Marnie really cared for her. Marnie was always stopping by to check on Rosemary and would bring her little gifts from time to time. Robb was nice to her as well, and she really liked him. But she felt connected to Marnie… so much so, more than her own children, that she had secretly amended her will and left her estate to Marnie and Robb. It wasn't much: the house was paid off, and she had some savings, but she wasn't rich by any means. She was okay, because she had always been frugal with money and she lived within her means. Her social security and pension was more than enough to live on each month, and so she rarely had to tap into savings.

She thought about the couple next door and hoped they would be safe. She scolded herself for worrying, but it was in her nature, especially if she cared about someone. She also missed them. It had only been a day, but she was used to the noise associated with neighbors, and it was way too quiet for her taste when they were away.

An idea struck her, and she went to the kitchen and rummaged around in the pantry for ingredients. Flour. Sugar. Chocolate chips. Nuts. Salt. Baking powder. She opened the refrigerator door. Eggs and butter. Check. She wouldn't have to run to the store after all. She would bake them a batch of cookies on Sunday and have them ready for them when they returned on Monday. She knew they would appreciate that.

Excited about her plan for the next day, Rosemary settled back into her chair and resumed reading her book. She became so engrossed in it that it wasn't until the light outside waned, making it hard for her to see the words, that she put the book down and made something to eat.

In the kitchen, she stared out the window at the lightless ones next door. Two days and they'd be home.

CHAPTER NINE

Chelle watched as Ms. Rachel taught her little audience about colors. Like many youngsters, Kayla was intrigued by the star of the show and always asked her mom to turn it on. Chelle didn't mind, because the content was so helpful in Kayla's development. Although she found the show to be slightly annoying, like most kids' shows, Chelle felt like Ms. Rachel could teach Kayla things that she herself wasn't able to.

How in the hell will Kayla ever grow up okay if you can't get your shit together?

The thought hit her like a freight train.

"You're right," she said out loud. "I need to get it together."

Kayla turned.

"What, Mommy?"

"Nothing, honey. Go back to your show."

Kayla turned back to watch the television, and Chelle opened up her social media app again to check her messages. The video from earlier hit her feed again. Her eyes glued to the screen, mesmerized as if she was watching it for the first time. It brought up feelings deep inside her that she hadn't felt for a long time. Hope. The possibility of something good happening.

When the video was over, she set the alarm on her phone to remind her about the live event the following day. She realized that the video really didn't explain what the event was that was scheduled for Sunday. Instead, the video simply urged people to attend. And something about it gave her a feeling of calm. Like everything was going to be okay.

As she mindlessly scrolled through her feed, she wondered what life would be like if she could pull herself out of the mire. If she could live a happy existence with Kayla by her side. If only she could be the positive role model Kayla so badly needed in her life. She wanted that. So badly. She just didn't know how to get there.

Kayla would be up several more hours. She'd let her watch Ms. Rachel as long as she wanted and then she'd feed her, give her a bath, and most likely zone out again. She wished she had a hobby, something to take her mind off her situation. Maybe even something that would heal her. But that would require her to care about something, and she just couldn't muster the strength.

Her phone rang. She looked at the number. It was her friend, Lisa. She let it go to voicemail. Lisa knew how badly she hated talking on the phone. It was her own fault though. She hadn't answered any of Lisa's texts in weeks. She knew what she wanted. For Chelle to get a sitter for the night and for them to go out and tear up the town. Only Chelle was in no condition to tear up anything.

As if reading her mind, Kayla turned to her.

"Look, Mommy. Ms. Rachel is talking about happy and sad. How come you aren't happy, Mommy? I only see you sad."

Chelle hung her head, a tear forming at the corner of her eye.

"C'mere, baby," she said. Chelle tapped her lap.

Kayla climbed up in the chair with Chelle and snuggled in.

"You make me very happy, pumpkin," Chelle told her, touching the tip of Kayla's nose with her pointer finger.

"Then how come you don't laugh anymore?"

Chelle paused, embarrassed by the question. Finally, she answered the best she could.

"It's hard to explain, baby. Mommy is just sad."

"Do I make you sad, Mommy?"

"No, baby, you make me happy!"

"Then why are you sad?"

"I'll explain it to you some day, baby girl. Just not tonight, okay?"

"Promise?"

"Pinky promise."

Chelle held out her pinky, and Kayla hooked her own pinky with her mom's.

"What's for dinner, Mommy?"

Relieved that Kayla had already changed the subject, she answered with, "What do you want for dinner?"

"Can we have chickee nuggies?"

"Yes, baby, we can have chickee nuggies. I'll do you one better. I'll take you to McDonald's and get you a Happy Meal."

"Yay!" Kayla squealed. "Thank you, Mommy!"

"Get your shoes on baby."

CHAPTER TEN

Robb pulled the last of the hamburger patties and hotdogs off the grill. Marnie had asked him why he was saving the old oven rack when they had remodeled their kitchen. She got her answer when he started a small fire, set the oven rack on top of the rocks surrounding the fire, and let the fire burn down a little before putting the meat on the rack.

They had brought frozen patties for convenience, and while Robb was cooking the meat, Joe got all the fixings ready to go, setting everything out on the fold-out table they had brought. The girls were sitting in lounge chairs nearby, not because they didn't want to help, but because the guys wanted to give them a break and cook a meal for them the first night. The Coronas went down smoothly, and the guys had even remembered the limes.

"Am I forgetting anything?" Joe asked. "I have the buns, cheese, onions, tomatoes, pickles, and lettuce for the burgers. We have ketchup, mustard, and mayo. Three kinds of chips and some potato salad that Marnie made."

"Sounds like you got it all," Robb said. "Oh wait… did you find the paper plates and napkins?"

"That might be helpful," Joe said, laughing.

The guys finished preparing the food and set everything out potluck style for everyone to dig in. Now, as they all sat around the fire eating, the mood was mellow, peaceful.

"This is *so* good," Marnie said.

"SO good," Emily echoed.

"It's amazing how the taste of something seems so different depending on where you are eating it," Joe said.

Rob agreed.

"I feel so relaxed," Emily said.

Marnie Smiled. "I thought I'd be going through social media withdrawals, but I'm actually happy to have the break. It's so much work keeping up with all of it."

"That and there are so many shit-posts." Robb shook his head.

"Yeah, a lot of negativity," Marnie said. "But the flip side is there are so many clever memes and videos. Some of them leave me laughing my ass off."

"Gotta take the bad with the good, I guess," Emily said.

"What do you guys want to do after we eat?" Marnie asked.

"We could play cards," Joe said. "Or…"

"Or?" Emily said.

"OR," Robb continued, "we can do movie night!"

"Movie night??" the girls said at the same time.

"Movie night!" the guys repeated in confirmation.

"How?" Marnie asked.

Joe smiled. "We set the tent doors facing the steep hill for a reason. So we can lay in our tents and watch movies."

"On?" Emily said.

"I downloaded some movies on my phone, and we bought a small projector that hooks right to the phone," Joe said. "It was a surprise."

Marnie play-hit Robb on the shoulder. "Is that what was in the mystery box?"

Robb smiled. "The screen, yeah. As long as we don't get any wind, we should be good."

"You guys are too much," Emily said.

"That better be a compliment," Joe said, laughing.

"Trust me, it is," Emily said, leaning over and kissing his lips.

Marnie felt like her smile was going to explode on her face. "Thanks, guys. This is the best trip ever."

"Ever!" Emily said.

They all finished eating, and after they had cleaned up, they got the screen and mini projector set up and retreated to their tents, the door flaps tied open. The evening cooled down a slight bit, making the weather perfect for cuddling in their sleeping bags while they watched movie after movie, well into the morning, and when no one was left awake, the movie played on, entertaining the crickets and other critters.

CHAPTER ELEVEN

His eyes snapped open. He sat up in his bed and looked around, disoriented. Within moments, the familiar surroundings had a calming effect on him, his breathing slowing down, his heartbeat eventually returning to normal.

Troy reached down and touched his shirt. It was soaked.

Fucking night terrors.

He had trouble falling asleep when he climbed into bed just after two a.m. His excitement for what the day held kept sleep at bay for several hours until he had passed out from pure exhaustion. Somewhere during his slumber, the terrors took him into their grip. He had experienced them before—probably because his mind was already fucked up—but nothing like these.

Everything had gone wrong. He was surrounded by chaos and disorder. But not in the catastrophic way he needed. He had failed big time.

He stripped off his damp clothes and dropped them on the floor, walking naked through his apartment to the bathroom. Under the hot stream of the showerhead, he let the stress leak from his body until he was fully relaxed.

After, he stood in front of the mirror, examining himself in the thin swipe of glass he had defogged with his palm. He knew he wasn't much to look at. Stupid hair. Thinner than he should be. But, to him anyway, he didn't look nearly as fucked up as he knew he was. People would be surprised if they found out who he really was. To him, his looks didn't matter… No one would want to be with him anyway.

The vanity vibrated. Troy looked down at his phone, the screen lit up fully. *THEM.*

Troy considered picking it up but decided against it. He imagined that the more calls he ignored, the more frantic his parents would be. Not that his intentions were to make them worry. He just didn't know what to say to them. And the questions… they were always excessive. Still, that same pang of guilt sliced at him. They hadn't done anything wrong to him… They were actually decent parents. They definitely deserved a better son than him. Unfortunately for them, he was their only child.

Congratulations, Mom and Dad. Your son is shithead of the century.

The phone went dark, the call parked again in voicemail. Another lengthy voicemail that he wouldn't listen to.

Sorry, Mom. Sorry, Dad.

He chose his clothing carefully. The nicest pair of jeans he owned. A button-down shirt. Looking at himself in the mirror, he thought he actually looked presentable—normal.

Running his fingers through his hair one last time, he sat down at his computer and booted up. The screens all came to life around him. He checked the engagement for the video he had released the prior day. He blinked when he saw the number. How was it even possible? He had over nine hundred ninety-seven million views.

Almost a fucking billion views? What the fuck? How many people are even on this planet?

Troy pulled up a web browser and did a search. Over eight billion people in the world. He had reached approximately an eighth of the world's population. Never in his wildest dreams did he think his algorithm would work that well.

Looking at the time, he noticed that there were only about eight hours left. He brought up his account and uploaded the next video, equally cryptic, yet sure to bring in more viewers. Troy watched the seconds tick by on his watch, an iWatch with a 3D gears-looking analog face.

Ten seconds.

Almost there.

Five seconds.

They'll wish they had treated me better.

One second.

Maybe this one will grab two billion.

Troy pressed ENTER, and the video uploaded and posted.

Eight hours 'til the main event.

With time to kill, Troy pulled out his phone and ordered food. It was time to feed.

CHAPTER TWELVE

The new video popped up on Chelle's phone at the top of her feed. The images that flashed pulled her attention immediately from the room, and she instantly was aware that the video was related to the one from the day before. The content didn't have a storyline. She didn't even remember what she had watched so far, nor what the video from the day before had contained. Rather, she only knew how it made her feel. Wanted. Hopeful. Loved.

Whole!

She devoured the entire five-minute visual and watched as it automatically cycled through a second time. When she pulled herself from her trance, unbeknownst to her, she had watched it eight times.

She took a deep breath to slow down the beating of her heart. A smile broke out on her face as she anticipated the event the next night. The event she knew she had to attend. She looked back at her screen to click the *Interested* button and noticed she had already pressed it. She didn't remember doing so.

She searched her emotions. What was this feeling? She had been depressed for so long that she didn't know anything else. Yet she felt euphoric. But several minutes ago, she had been stuck in her chamber of despair. She dared to hope, but only a little. If the event later in the evening—whatever it turned out to be—was everything her soul wanted it to be, it would be life altering.

A small part of her felt foolish. This was social media. Most of it was garbage. Surely, she was getting amped up over nothing. But as quickly as the negative thoughts emerged, she replayed the video, and the thoughts vanquished themselves from her consciousness.

"Mommy?"

Chelle tuned her attention to Kayla.

"Hi, baby girl."

"Can I have ice cream?"

"It's a little early for ice cream, baby."

"Please, Mommy?" Kayla looked up at Chelle with her big, beautiful blue eyes.

Chelle smiled. "Ugh. You have me wrapped around your little finger, don't you?"

Kayla smiled and nodded. Chelle went to the freezer and got out the Rocky Road ice cream. She took a bowl out of the cupboard and set it next to the ice cream, reconsidered, and returned to the cupboard for a second bowl. When she had dished out both bowls, she set them at the kitchen table.

"We have to eat at the table, little one, so we don't make a mess."

"Okay, Mommy."

Kayla sat down, and Chelle pulled up the chair next to hers.

"You found your smile again, Mommy!" Kayla said, looking up at her mother's face.

"It appears I did, honey."

"You're really pretty, Mommy."

Chelle felt her smile practically split her face in half.

"You're really pretty too, baby girl!"

"Thank you, Mommy!"

They ate their ice cream, and Chelle giggled at the chocolate mustache that adorned Kayla's lip. Chelle grabbed a napkin off the table and wiped Kayla's mouth.

"Can we watch a movie after this, Mommy?"

Chelle let out a content sigh.

"Let's do it. You even get to pick."

CHAPTER THIRTEEN

Rosemary mixed the ingredients in the bowl and stirred. It was mid-day Sunday, and she knew the kids would be heading home sometime the next day. She hoped they didn't leave too late… She wanted them to get home while it was still light outside. Their drive would be safer that way. Plus, she wanted to make sure they received their cookies right when they got back.

When the mixture was just right, she spooned table-spoons full of the batter onto the wax-paper-covered cookie sheets, and when the oven beeped signaling the preheating had finished, she opened the oven door and slid the two sheets onto the middle rack. She then set the timer on the stove and sat on one of the kitchen barstools, switching between reading paragraphs of her current book and glancing at the timer, making sure she didn't leave the cookies in too long. She had never burned cookies before, and she wasn't about to start now.

When the timer finally went off, she pulled the two

cookie sheets out, placed them on cooling racks, and slid the last two cookie sheets into the oven. When those were finished, she pulled them out to cool down as well.

After the last of the cookie dough was baked, Rosemary got comfortable in her recliner and read some more. She would get the cookies ready to go to the kids that evening, after they had cooled down.

She hoped that Robb and Marnie were safe. Marnie had tried to explain where they were going, but never having been, Marnie hadn't been able to give Rosemary an adequate description. Still, it brought back memories of when Rosemary had gone camping when she was younger, and she smiled at the flashbacks. She had mostly great memories of her trips with her parents or her friends with only a few catastrophes. Regardless of whether Robb and Marnie had the time of their lives or not, at least they weren't stuck at home where absolutely nothing was happening.

CHAPTER FOURTEEN

Clifford and Mary Berodach sat on their patio in Anthem, Arizona, enjoying the warm day while they drank their Arnold Palmers. Clifford fussed with his crossword puzzle, and when he finally pulled his attention away and toward Mary, he caught her staring at her phone again.

"Staring at it isn't going to make him call."

"I just don't get it."

"He's young. Parents aren't important at his age."

"Still… I'm worried, Cliff."

"He can take care of himself. Why are you so worried?"

"He's never gone this long without answering our calls."

"I'm sure he's fine."

"But what if he's not? What if he's hurt? There would be no one to help him."

"Troy doesn't seem like the type to get himself in a situation where he was left helpless."

"He also doesn't seem like the type not to at least call his parents back. I've left at least six messages."

"You've been on this for days, Mary. Relax. He'll call when he calls."

"And how are you going to feel if we don't do something and he's hurt?"

"What are you going to do, Mary? He's three thousand miles away. Are you going to hop a plane?"

"I'm tempted."

"Jesus," Clifford said.

"I'm not like you. I can't just ignore things… can't just push my feelings down."

"Okay, fine. What do you want to do? Maybe after you find out he's just fine, you'll stop all this nonsense."

"Yes, Clifford." Her voice was dripping with frustration. "Me with all my nonsense. You can tell me I was freaking out for nothing once we hear from him. I'll let you have that one."

"Ideas? Should we call his landlord or something?" Clifford asked.

"I don't have that information."

"Police? Wellness check? Seems like overkill."

"Better safe than sorry."

"Just don't call 911. We'll find the non-emergency line."

"That'll be your job," she said.

"If it'll get you to relax, then I'm on it."

CHAPTER FIFTEEN

Joe handed drinks to the others sitting in the pond and worked his way back into his chair. They had been sitting there for a couple of hours soaking up the late afternoon sun.

"I never want this weekend to end," Emily said.

"Me either," Marnie agreed.

"Sad we have to leave tomorrow," Robb chimed in.

"I knew you guys would love it here," Joe said.

"Hard to think of going camping anywhere else now," Marnie said.

"No reason to go anywhere else now," Joe added.

They had slept longer than they had thought they would. It was when the sun was up for a while and the tents had started warming up that they had pulled themselves out of their sleeping bags and cooked a nice camp-fire breakfast.

Now, after an afternoon of drinking and snacking, the day was winding down.

"What time do you think we should head out tomorrow?" Robb asked Joe.

"I wouldn't mind getting home at a decent hour to get the gear put away and settle in before going back to work on Tuesday."

"So maybe just get up whenever we get up, eat, then break down camp and hit the road?"

"Yeah, probably."

Robb turned toward the girls. "Does that work for you guys?"

"As long as I don't have to get up at the ass-crack of dawn, I'm good," Marnie said.

"Same," Emily said.

They hung out in the water for a while longer, but when the sun started slipping farther down the cotton-candy-clouded skies, Marnie stood up and got out of the water.

"I'm getting hungry," she said. "Anyone else?"

"I could eat," Emily said. "Shall we cook tonight?"

"Only fair."

Emily stood from her chair and got out of the water, adjusting her bikini top as she did. At the tent area, she grabbed a towel and started drying off, joining Marnie, who already had a towel wrapped around her. Moments later, the guys moved to chairs nearby, also deciding it was time to get out of the water. The guys watched as the girls cooked, their hunger building by the minute.

CHAPTER SIXTEEN

Officer Ashley Cummins sat in her patrol car by the side of the road, bored. She spent an hour unsuccessfully looking for speeders, but no one was driving fast enough to interest her. She usually gave drivers grace for nine miles an hour over or less, but none of them exceeded that range.

Now, she was scrolling through her social media. It was almost quarter to six, and she had received an invitation for a mysterious event. Since she was working, she hadn't gotten her hopes up that she'd be able to attend. It always seemed like calls came in when she least wanted them to. Still, she was intrigued, and since it was getting close, maybe she'd be able to catch some of the event after all.

The radio sounded.

"Car forty-five, ten sixty-three."

"Fucking figures," she muttered. She keyed the mic. "Forty-five go ahead."

"Requesting a wellness check for a Troy Berodach of 1254 Highland Street. Apartment number is twenty-three."

Ashley sighed and turned off the screen on her phone, storing it on her belt.

"Forty-five enroute. Will advise."

Sliding the gearshift into drive, Ashley headed toward the apartment complex, which was approximately ten minutes away. Scenarios ran through her head as she never knew what she was going to find during a wellness check. Most of the time, there was no issue. Occasionally, she found the dreaded dead body. Some natural deaths, some suicides, and of course the occasional murder. And the fucking maggots. Ashley didn't do maggots. One sign of them and she was outside calling for backup.

Pulling into the parking lot, she found a place to park her cruiser in front of a dumpster, got out, locked up the car, and headed toward the apartment in question.

CHAPTER SEVENTEEN

Chelle washed the dishes that were in the sink and looked at the time on the microwave. It was five minutes to six, and Kayla had already eaten and taken a bath. Chelle put Kayla in her room and put on a movie, bribing her with a special treat the next day if she was good and stayed in her bed.

The dishes done, Chelle dried off her hands and climbed into her favorite chair. She reached into her back pocket and pulled out her phone. Two minutes until the event. She felt her heartrate accelerate. Whatever was going to happen was going to be epic. She would bet her life on it.

CHAPTER EIGHTEEN

One of Troy's huge monitors had a doomsday clock displayed on it, taking up the entire monitor. The countdown timer showed ninety seconds left. He glanced at the right-hand monitor and checked for the fifth time that the event was ready to be published.

Eighty seconds. Troy wiped the sweat from his right palm onto his jeans.

A hard rap sounded at the door. Troy's attention was pulled to it.

"Who the fuck could that be and why now?"

He whipped his attention back to the timer. Sixty-nine seconds. No time to get distracted.

The knock came again. This time, firmer, louder. "Police department."

Again, his eyes darted toward the door and back.

The fucking police? What?

Sixty seconds.

"Troy Berodach. This is the Evergreen Police Department. Can we talk?"

Troy's mouth dropped open.

How could they know?

He wondered how long he could stall them. What if he didn't answer? Would they simply leave?

Troy's eyes darted between the door, the doomsday clock, and the button.

"Mr. Berodach?"

The knock sounded louder this time.

"Evergreen Police Department!"

Thirty-five seconds.

He internally chastised himself for not scheduling the event to run automatically, but he understood why he hadn't. It would have taken away the sense of satisfaction, the feeling of power.

He watched the door for a bit, not knowing what he expected to see or hear.

Troy looked at the clock. Ten seconds.

The front door swung open, and Troy's mouth fell open. How the fuck had he failed to lock the door? Standing in the doorframe was a female cop. His mind flashed, unable to process what was happening. He stood frozen for a few seconds and then glanced at the clock.

"Mr. Berodach?"

Three seconds. Two. One.

Troy launched himself at the enter button and pressed it, inadvertently noticing the light gun gaming controller —he had spent so much time finding one that looked realistic—sitting next to his keyboard, his mind thinking the words *OH SHIT*, the moment exploding into an overload of sounds, light, smells, and finally pain. It was only when he was crumpled on the floor that he realized he had heard gunfire, that he actually smelled gunpowder.

He looked down at his shirt, the red blooming at a rapid pace. The cop called for assistance on her radio. His senses began to swim, and he felt tired. So tired.

I did it. I pushed the button. It's happening.

As he faded to black, he realized that he wasn't going to be around to watch the aftermath. He felt robbed, his satisfaction stripped from him.

"Fuck me," he whispered as his eyes closed forever.

CHAPTER NINETEEN

Chelle watched as the event went live. Another video. Flashes of different incoherent scenes, but she couldn't look away. In fact, the video had the opposite effect. It was mesmerizing. The stress left her body. Euphoria replaced it.

She stared at the screen for the full five minutes, barely blinking, enlightened for the first time in her life. Then the video ended abruptly and disappeared as if it had never existed.

Chelle blinked and stood up. She walked into the bathroom, pushed down the tub stopper, and turned on the water. As the tub filled, she slid off her clothes, letting them fall into a pile on the floor.

The water finally reached the max level and water started sloshing down the overflow drain. Chelle shut it off.

She opened the door and went to the kitchen, still

completely nude. In the bottom junk drawer, she grabbed an extension cord, then unplugged the toaster and brought it into her embrace.

Just outside the bathroom, she plugged the extension cord into the hall outlet and plugged the toaster into it, entering the small room and setting it on the corner edge of the tub. She slipped her foot into the water, and when it adjusted to the temperature, she fully climbed in and slid her body under the water.

She smiled, knowing, understanding.

A meme flashed into her head as she reached over with her toes and pulled the toaster into the bathwater.

LIVE. LAUGH. TOASTER BATH.

Paul Hoffman was halfway through his lunch hour when the video ended. He stood up from the table in the break room.

"Paul, are you okay?" Megan, a coworker, asked.

There was no response. She tried again.

"What's with that shit-eating grin on your face?"

Paul never turned her direction. Instead, he exited the breakroom. Megan shook her head and turned her attention back to the book she was reading for a second, and then it hit her. She whipped her head back up and looked at the others in the room that held ten tables. Out of the fifteen or so people in the room, ten of them were standing up, the same type of look on their faces, a mix of guys and girls.

"What are you guys doing?" Megan called out to the room.

As before, she got no response. Then, as she watched, they all single-filed out of the room and onto the production floor.

Megan wondered if they weren't playing some kind of stupid joke. She called to the girl at the next table.

"Did you see that?"

"Yeah. Weird."

"Very."

Megan got up from the table and exited into the hallway. She could just see the last of the group turning the corner ahead of her. She walked down the hallway slowly, cautiously, as if the boogeyman was going to jump out at her at any moment.

When she finally rounded the next corner, she saw the last one climbing the stairs to the catwalk, and bells and whistles went off in her head.

At the plant they worked at, one of the products they produced was made from ground-up tires. They had six of the humongous machines in the one room, which had a catwalk built around the upper level of the room, almost like an observation deck where anyone could watch the machines in action. Several conveyers fed the machine, and then the output landed on a different belt, carting off the altered material to the next phase of manufacturing.

Megan called out to the guy at the end of the pack, but again, there was no response, and he disappeared through the door at the top. Megan ran up the stairs, the intense volume of the machines masking any noise she made. She got to the door, paused for a second, and pulled it open.

Not knowing what to expect, she knew it was anything but what she saw before her. Her mouth worked as she tried to call out, but no sound came out. Not that she could probably have been heard over the extreme volume anyway.

Helpless, she watched as the guy and girl at the end of the line fell face forward over the safety railing and right into the steel jaws of two of the machines. There was a spray of blood from both apparatuses that shot up three feet in the air, and fluid and gristle coated the machines and the area around them, joining the carnage from the others that jumped in before them.

Megan tried to hold back her purge, but it was too much for her, and she projectile vomited her lunch over the railing, the spew joining the rest of the chunky mess below. Her legs betrayed her, and she sank to the floor of the catwalk, where management would find her minutes later when they came to investigate the gore they received on the output belt.

ADAM SANDERSON THOUGHT HE WAS BEING SNEAKY. He sat on the couch with phone in hand, three minutes to spare. He had been waiting all day to check out the event, and it figured that Janine and her perfect (not) fucking timing would strike again.

Janine entered the living room, a mischievous smile on her face. She was wearing a thin t-shirt, her nipples stiff and visible through the fabric. Her shorts were extremely small, and Adam sucked in his breath, the reaction he always had when she walked into the room.

Janine had a habit of always teasing him, but then she always gave it up immediately after. He was a lucky man, and he never turned her down, but he cursed her timing. This event was extremely important to him, so he cheated. When she was standing directly in front of him and peeled her t-shirt off, exposing her expensive breasts, Adam quickly changed the setting on the TV to mirror his phone, and he turned it face down on the couch cushion next to him.

Now, with her back to the TV, Janine pulled her hair back and dropped to her knees, sliding Adam's basketball shorts around his ankles. As she slid his erect penis in her mouth, Adam shuddered and then laid back and enjoyed both forms of entertainment. Hopefully she wouldn't catch him watching the television. If she did, it'd be a while until his next blowjob.

Her mouth was skilled. He couldn't remember ever having another partner that could get him off with their mouth. Janine was the only one that could pull it off.

As he watched the video, his vision tunneled, and he no longer noticed Janine before him on her knees. All he saw were the images in the video, and he associated the pleasure from the blowie as pleasure that was coming from the video. As he watched, he felt his orgasm building and he knew it wouldn't be long. His eyes wanted to roll up in the back of his head, but he fought to keep his attention locked on the television.

The video neared the end and so did he. He felt the pressure build and his toes curled. He moaned as he shot his full load into Janine's mouth. As skilled as she was, she didn't spill a drop.

As Janine greedily tried to squeeze any remaining bounty from her prize, the video disappeared off the screen, and Adam abruptly stood up, almost causing Janine's teeth to scrape his member. He didn't care.

"Babe, what the fuck!"

Adam walked toward the bedroom, a smile plastered on his face.

"ADAM!"

He didn't answer, didn't turn around. He continued his walk down the hallway to the bedroom.

"Oh, are we playing bedroom games?" she asked, giggling and getting up off the floor to follow him.

Adam walked into the bedroom and opened his bedside table drawer. Janine followed him into the room. As she started to round the corner of the bed to come up behind him, he reached into the drawer, pulled out a pistol, flicked off the safety, slid the gun into his open mouth, and pulled the trigger.

Janine watched as the wall and curtain behind him became a bloody Jackson Pollock painting. She screamed, unable to fathom what had just transpired in front of her. Sinking to her knees, deep gasping sobs escaped from her body, and she became a useless puddle of flesh and bone. It would be a good twenty minutes before she could work up the strength to call 911.

MISTY RUTHERFORD WAS BORED, AND SHE KNEW SHE shouldn't have been. South Mission Beach in San Diego, California, was a beautiful place to be, and the weather was delightful. It was in the mid-seventies.

As she sat on the large blanket, she fixed her bikini top and brushed some sand off her belly that was sticking to the sunscreen. She looked around at the hundreds of people milling around. No one caught her interest.

At seventeen, Misty was at that stage where she liked to hang out with her friends, but hanging out with her family was cringe. Her parents had planned this big *surprise* day for her and her siblings, and the five of them traveled over two hours to get there.

Now her parents were off on a long walk down the shoreline, undoubtably collecting broken sand dollars and any other shells they saw that hadn't been scooped up by other beachgoers that acted like they had never seen a seashell before. Her siblings? Well, who knew where they were. At fifteen, the twins, Steve and Staci, were running around having the time of their life. They hadn't started driving yet, so they didn't know the freedom that Misty felt every time she got behind the wheel. They didn't understand that the best times were to be had hanging with friends, not hanging out with boring family.

And here she was, left all alone on the huge beach blanket, wishing she was with her boyfriend, the boyfriend she had been dating for a year and really liked… the boyfriend that she had promised she would spend the day with, because he had to work the next day.

As hard as she tried to wrangle out of the trip to the coast and as much as she begged and pleaded with her parents, they insisted she come, spouting some bullshit about her almost being eighteen and who knew when their last trip as a family would be. After an hour of arguing about it and another half hour of ugly-crying in her room, she finally conceded, texted Billy, her boyfriend, and packed a day bag.

Now she sat alone, bored. The rest of her family was doing their own thing, and she actually felt relieved over that fact. If she wasn't dating Billy, she'd probably be checking out the boys, but since she met him, she had no interest in anyone else.

Misty pulled her phone out of her bag. She checked her social media, and as she was scrolling, a video caught her attention. Typically, it was not her style as there was no plot, but she couldn't look away. For five minutes, she was mesmerized, but then the screen faded to black.

Misty dropped the phone on the blanket and stood up. Unaware of her actions, she started walking toward the water, also unaware that thirty-seven other people on the crowded beach were making the same death walk.

The beach turned chaotic as people started to notice what was going on. Loved ones asked their family members where they were going. No answers were given as thirty-eight people walked toward the water, almost as if in a trance. One guy tried to physically stop his girl-friend, and with lightning speed, she leg swept him and knocked him to the sand before he knew what was happening. She had no training in martial arts.

As the group started into the water, some swam out into the depths. Some were deterred by loved ones, which led to physical altercations. One teenager was carried to the sand, kicking and screaming, by four of her guy friends.

No one from Misty's family noticed her, and she was able to slip into the water and start swimming. Her body took her where her brain told it to go. For all practical purposes, her mind or will were not part of the equation. Then, when she was out far enough, she stopped swimming and slipped beneath the surface like a stone.

GREG WORMWOOD AND HIS THREE FRIENDS, BRIAN, Darian, and Paul, were all hanging out in the basement of his parents' home. They had spent the morning playing baseball and had gone out to lunch after. Now, they were just hanging out and watching movies.

"Guys, have you seen anything about this event today online?" Greg said. "Everyone's attending. Look at these numbers. Over a billion attendees."

"No fucking way," Paul said.

"I'm serious."

The boys all crowded around Greg on the couch.

"Start the video," Darian said.

"Can't. It's a live event, but it starts in a minute."

"What is it about?" Brian said.

"No clue," Greg said. "I just stumbled across it. I'm

reading the comments though. Seems like the event of the century."

The video started and the boys watched, oblivious. Silence overtook the room except for the sound accompanying the video. When the video finished, they all filed upstairs single file and entered the kitchen. Greg walked over to the butcher block and slid out the biggest knife he could find and passed it to Brian, who passed it to the end of the line. Greg repeated the process two more times and then selected a knife of his own. A meaningful glance was exchanged amongst them, but no words were spoken.

With a single nod, the boys all turned toward the one closest to them and drew the sharp blades across the other boy's neck. Four slices, all in one single synchronized motion. The damage done, they all dropped the knives to the floor, the blood spurting from four necks, essentially redecorating the white cabinets with a dash of color.

The boys tried to remain standing as long as they could, but one by one, they fell into heaps on the floor. It would be hours before Greg's mom would be home from work and discover the carnage.

PROFESSOR HUDSON SHUSHED THE CLASS.

"Okay, so as we talked about at the beginning of class

today, we are just going to have some fun. Consider this a social experiment. Not sure how it's going to go, but we'll wing it.

"So basically, the event happens in a couple minutes, and we will watch it as a group in its entirety on the projector screen. When it's over, we'll all take turns talking about it and how it made us feel. If you participate, you get full points for today's assignment. If you don't participate, you get a zero."

Jennifer Hudson had been a professor for six years and had taught developmental psychology for the last two. She had a reputation around campus as being one of the "fun teachers," mostly because of her non-traditional teaching methods and her out-of-the-box thinking. Her class roster was always full, and attendance was unusually high. To put it simply, the kids didn't like to skip her class.

She connected her phone to the projector by Bluetooth and brought up the event, watching a timer count down the last thirty seconds. Picking up a small remote, she dimmed the lights.

The video started playing, and at first, many of the students looked around at each other, but within seconds, the video had their full attention.

For almost the full five minutes, not one eye was averted from the screen. Not one word was spoken. No one was distracted. The message was received loud and clear.

When the video was over, Professor Hudson blinked and walked over to one of the big windows on the south wall. She unlocked the latch and pushed on the glass, which swung out, leaving a fairly large opening.

Two of the biggest guys stood up from the rows of desks and walked to the windows, helpers, pawns. They knew what to do.

One of the female students broke into a run toward the boys, and as she got within reach of them, they joined hands and created a springboard for her to pounce from. She pushed off of their hands while they flung her toward the window, her arms straight forward in a diving pose.

Their aim was awkward, and her head bounced off the frame of the top part of the window before she flipped out of the window and fell the three stories to the concrete below. The next student came running, and this time, they were able to help fling the kid straight out the window with no frame contact.

One by one, the students came running, and one by one, they all were launched out the window. When no one else was left but her and the two boys, she ran to them for her turn.

Everyone's getting an A, was the only thought that ran through her mind.

AFTER A FILLING MEAL OF PULLED PORK SANDWICHES and corn on the cob, they sat around the fire feeling sluggish and happy.

"What time is it?" Robb asked.

Marnie grabbed her phone off the table, an expensive paperweight in their current environment.

"It's six o'clock on the dot," she said.

Robb gave a relaxed sigh. "At six back home, the traffic would be horrendous. But here… just listen."

"So quiet," Emily said.

"It is," Joe agreed. "As if the world doesn't even exist."

"Like we're the only ones alive," Marnie said.

CHAPTER TWENTY

Rosemary had the front door open to let in the fresh air, but if she were being honest with herself, it was so she could hear when the neighbor's truck pulled into the driveway. The past few days had been boring, and she was excited they were coming home.

She put her book down and turned on the television. The news was on, which she didn't usually watch, so she turned the channel. Another news story dominated that channel as well. She switched channels again and then saw the start of a breaking news broadcast.

What's going on?

Rosemary turned up the volume, so she could hear what they were saying.

ANCHOR:

Good evening. We begin tonight with breaking news that has sent shockwaves around the world. Authorities are working tirelessly to determine the full extent of a rapidly unfolding situation. Early reports suggest that a large number of deaths have occurred globally, with eyewitnesses citing a disturbing trend: many of the victims appear to have died by suicide.

While it's still too soon to confirm the exact scope of this tragedy, reports continue to flood in, with some estimates suggesting the death toll could reach into the millions.

The central question remains: What is causing this? To help shed some light on the situation, we are joined now by Chantelle Cassidy, a medical. sociologist and expert on mass psychogenic illnesses. Thank you for joining us on such short notice, Chantelle.

CHANTELLE CASSIDY (Medical Sociologist):

Thank you for having me.

ANCHOR:

Chantelle, with so many deaths occurring simultaneously around the world, many of them by suicide, what's your initial assessment of this situation?

CHANTELLE CASSIDY:

First, Ron, I'd like to express my deepest condolences to all those affected by this tragedy. It's clear that this event is impacting countless families, and its ripple effects will be felt worldwide.

At this stage, it's difficult to determine the precise cause, but based on the information we've seen so far, it does appear to be some sort of mass psychogenic event.

ANCHOR:

Mass psychogenic event? Could you explain that term and what it might mean in this context?

CHANTELLE CASSIDY:

Certainly. In more typical cases, we might refer to this as mass hysteria. However, given the scale and the synchronized nature of the events we're seeing, that doesn't seem to fully explain the situation. What's particularly alarming is that, according to witnesses, people across the globe seemingly stopped whatever they were doing and simultaneously began engaging in self-harm. This suggests something far more deliberate, possibly even a form of brainwashing or hypnosis. It's possible that some kind of external programming could have played a role here.

ANCHOR:

What do you mean by "programming," Chantelle? Could you expand on that?

CHANTELLE CASSIDY:

For an event like this to unfold on such a massive scale, there would have to be some sort of message or influence implanted within people's minds. This could have been done subliminally, perhaps over a period of time. While it's still early in the investigation, I believe this is one avenue that authorities will need to explore further.

ANCHOR:

We've just received reports indicating that many of the victims were reportedly on an unknown social media platform just before they took their own lives. Do you think there could be a link between this platform and the events we're seeing unfold?

CHANTELLE CASSIDY:

It's difficult to draw definitive conclusions at this point, but for such a widespread event to impact so many people, there must have been a medium capable of reaching a global audience. In my view, the internet —particularly social media—has the kind of reach necessary to influence such a large portion of the population.

ANCHOR:

It's certainly a chilling thought. Thank you again, Chantelle, for your insights. We know you'll be monitoring this closely as the investigation continues, and we hope to have you back with us soon for further updates.

CHANTELLE CASSIDY:

Thank you for having me. I look forward to discussing this further as we learn more.

Rosemary sat in silence as she watched the newscast, confused, her hand to her head. She didn't understand what was happening, but she was mostly concerned for the kids, her next-door neighbors. Since they were really the only family she had, she wondered what would happen to her if something had happened to them.

Her attention flipped back to the television.

ANCHOR:

We've just received reports confirming that a nationwide state of emergency has been declared. As a precautionary measure, authorities have temporarily shut down access to the World Wide Web. While the duration of this disruption remains unclear, all internet-based platforms, including mobile applications, are expected to be offline. In an increasingly digital world, this shutdown could have devastating effects on remote work, e-commerce, and global supply chains. We will continue to monitor the situation closely and provide updates as more information becomes available.

Rosemary grabbed a tissue from the box sitting on the table beside the chair. She dabbed at her eyes, a tightness in her chest and a fog in her brain. She wasn't able to understand the totality of what she had just heard. She didn't have internet, so she had no idea about that either. But she was scared, and a heavy sense of foreboding hung in the air. She wondered what happened and if this was the end of everything she ever knew.

CHAPTER TWENTY-ONE

"Where is all the traffic?" Marnie asked.

Marnie and Robb had followed Joe and Emily down the mountain. Now, they were all sitting outside a gas station in the town they had lunch in at the start of their trip. The gas station appeared to be closed.

"It's eerie," Emily agreed.

"Gas station isn't even open," Joe added.

"*Nothing* looks open," Robb said.

"Fucking small towns," Joe said.

"How are you guys doing on gas?" Marnie asked. "We have plenty if you just want to hit the interstate and stop along the way at a truck stop or something."

"We're good," Emily said.

"Yeah, and I'm not really hungry, but we have plenty to snack on," Robb said.

"Same," Joe said. "Let's hit the road."

CHAPTER TWENTY-TWO

Officer Ashley Cummins sped toward her home in her patrol car, lights flashing. Typically, she wouldn't use the patrol car for personal business, but she was scared.

After the officer-involved shooting—this was her

first time shooting someone, let alone killing them—Ashley followed protocol and called in the incident. She was surprised when she got no reply but was completely shocked when no one arrived on scene. She even tried dialing 911 and calling her direct supervisor's cellphone.

Finally, after an hour of waiting, and all out of options, Ashley secured the scene and drove to the station. She had no idea what was happening, but she knew there was nothing good about the situation.

At the station, she noticed most of the patrol cars were missing. Inside, she found no one around the station, so she made her way to dispatch. The room was empty, but then Ashley spotted one of the ladies who worked there laying on the ground beside her chair, blood trickling from a substantial wound in the side of her head. A gun lay nearby. Ashley covered her mouth, gasped, then quickly recovered, pulling her gun from its holster. She meticulously cleared the station room by room. There were no other people in the station.

Cautiously, Ashley entered the dispatch room again and looked around, the discord of unanswered calls coming through as a torrential downpour of noise. The radio chatter was incoherent as multiple units tried to talk over each other. Ashley picked up the mic and tried to broadcast the situation at the station. She got no response. But as she listened to the chatter on the radio, she was able to make out a common theme to the chaos. Dead bodies. Everywhere. Suicide. Some sort of Jim Jones Kool-Aid drinking shit without the Kool-Aid.

Ashley thought about Troy Berodach. The wellness check that went badly. He had put himself in harm's way to push that button on his keyboard. And although it was probably coincidence, everything went to shit immediately after. From what she gathered, there were hundreds of casualties. Maybe thousands.

For the first time as a police officer, she didn't know what to do. She had killed a person. Possibly innocent. She had left the scene, although she could not stay there forever if no one was responding. People lay dead everywhere from what she was hearing. She had no idea where to go or what to do and no direction from a supervisor.

Ashley's daughters popped into her mind. At ten and twelve, one was still in that stage of being Mommy's sweet little girl while the other was finding her sassy side. Were they safe in all of this? She called her husband. The call rang through to voicemail. She tried again with no response and left a message, following it up with a text for him to call her immediately. And then she tried both of her daughters' phones and got no response from them either.

Trying to create a reporting timestamp, Ashley composed a text to her boss's cell phone. She informed him of the officer-involved shooting, the steps she took, how long she waited, and what she found at the station. She also added her thoughts on Troy Berodach possibly having some involvement with whatever was happening around them.

After she sent the text, she tried her husband again. Four more rings and it went to voicemail. Her stomach clenched up tight, and her body grew tense. Cop or no cop, she had to check on her family. They were possibly the only thing she had left in life since her career had probably been flushed down the toilet.

Now, a couple of miles from her house, the world felt different. A couple cars had crashed here and there, but no activity existed at the crash sites. Other vehicles were just stopped in the middle of the road. Ashley noticed a body at the bus stop and another laying on the sidewalk. Was this it? Was this the apocalypse?

Finally, Ashley rounded the corner to her street and pulled up into their driveway. Everything seemed fairly normal in her neighborhood, albeit quiet and still. She left the car halfway in the driveway and half on the street, the lights flashing, and fumbled with her key in the lock. Pushing through the front door, Ashley noticed the TV on but did not see her children or her husband. In the bedroom, she finally found Michael. Her heart exploded as her worst fear was realized. Michael lay, crumpled on the floor, unmoving, his wrists slit, his blood soaked into the carpet. Ashley sniffled, trying to put on a brave face for her children. She called out their names, and when she got no answer, she searched through the rest of the house. Not finding them, she opened the vertical blinds that covered the sliding glass door leading to the back-yard. The glass door was already open. Ashley's heart felt like it was going to explode in her chest, and as much as she tried to tell herself not to freak out—not yet—she already knew. Stepping outside, her eyes immediately went to the pool. She didn't need to look any further. Floating in the deep end were her daughters, Mia and Emma.

Ashley dropped to the concrete patio, the contents of her utility belt slamming into the hard, unforgiving surface. A tear slipped down from the corner of her eye. Her entire world had ended. Her beautiful children, gone. Her husband and best friend, gone. Her career, gone. Life on this planet as she knew it, gone. With zero hesitation, Ashley removed her service pistol from its holster and put it up under her chin.

See you on the other side, my loves.

CHAPTER TWENTY-THREE

Rosemary heard the unmistakable sound of the truck. It was then she realized just how vulnerable she really was. She had nothing tying her to this world, and if the kids had not come back, she would not have wanted to plow through every day on this godforsaken planet with no purpose.

Rosemary got up and exited the side door, waving at them as they pulled into the driveway. Robb hastily parked the truck and they both scurried out, making their way over to Rosemary.

"We are so glad you're okay," Marnie said.

"Yes, we were worried about you," Robb said.

"I was extremely worried about the both of you as well," Rosemary said. "Any idea what's going on?"

"We were hoping you would know," Robb said. "There is next to no traffic on the roads, most businesses seem to be closed, and we can't seem to connect to the internet to research it."

Rosemary frowned. "They've taken the internet down," she said.

"What do you mean, taken it down?" Marty said. "Who is they?"

"The authorities," Rosemary said.

"Is there anything on the news?" Robb said.

"A bunch of people are dead. Hundreds. Thousands. Probably more. I don't know."

"Let's go inside and watch the news… Is that okay?" Robb asked.

"Yes, dears, come in."

CHAPTER TWENTY-FOUR

Robb pulled the car into a parking spot at the old school. They were driving Rosemary's Subaru Forester.

"Ready?" Marnie asked.

"As ready as I'll ever be," Robb said.

Marnie turned toward the back seat and addressed Rosemary.

"You coming in with us?"

"I think I'll wait in the car. I don't want to overwhelm the poor dear."

Rosemary watched as Robb and Marnie walked inside the building, holding hands.

In the three months since the event that came to be known as "The Reckoning," they had all become very close. The fragility of life had become all too apparent. They spent most evenings together, and together, they had put an offer in on a home that would comfortably hold all of them and still give Rosemary some space and independence. When it closed, they would all move in together and sell their current houses.

Rosemary thought about all that had transpired since that fateful day. Over one billion dead… almost an eighth of the world's population. All at the hands of a madman named Troy Berodach.

The internet was taken down for a few weeks during the investigation. When they brought it back up, they permanently banned social media sites simultaneously.

Life had certainly changed since then. Nations mourned. Families were torn apart. Children were left orphaned.

Rosemary's thoughts were interrupted by Robb and Marnie walking out of the building, a school that had been converted to an orphanage. Between them, holding their hands, walked Kayla.

At the car, they introduced her to Rosemary.

"Kayla, this is Grandma Rosemary."

"Hello."

Kayla smiled timidly and climbed into the back seat next to Rosemary.

After The Reckoning had taken place, Robb and Marnie had heard Kayla's story. Kayla had found her mom in the bathtub, dead, and had the instinct to seek out a neighbor for help. Since then, Kayla had learned her father was dead also. The little girl was left with no family and was placed at one of the newly designated orphanages that had popped up all over the country.

Robb and Marnie had visited her many times and fell in love with her, finally deciding to fill out the adoption paperwork. The process had been streamlined, another necessity after The Reckoning. There were plenty of children that needed homes, and thousands of people volunteered their time to tirelessly make it happen.

"Your bedroom is all ready for you, Sweetie. Are you ready to go home?" Marnie asked.

"Yes, please," she said, her eyes cast downward.

"Is there anything you need?" Marnie asked.

"Can we get a puppy?"

Marnie, Robb, and Rosemary laughed, her request a simple one. An innocent one. A necessary one.

Marnie looked at Robb, and he nodded.

"Of course, honey. We can go tomorrow and find you a puppy."

Kayla giggled and threw her hands up in the air.

"I can gets a puppy? Really?"

"Really! So you better start picking out a name!"

Kayla squealed with delight and thanked them over and over, also asking questions about her new home. Eventually, the excitement caught up with her over the four-hour drive, and she fell asleep.

The road stretched ahead, endless and uncertain, much like the new world they were navigating. Robb kept one hand steady on the wheel, the other resting in Marnie's lap, her fingers curled around his. In the back-seat, Rosemary sat beside Kayla, the little girl asleep against her shoulder, her tiny breaths a quiet reminder that life, however changed, still moved forward. No one spoke much—there were no words for what had been lost, for how different everything now felt—but in the hum of the tires against the pavement, in the warmth of familiar hands and the presence of those who remained, there was something close to hope. The world would never be the same, but as long as they had each other, they would find their way.

Join the Crystal Lake community today!

Subscribe to our Newsletter!
(Scan the QR code or click if eBook)

Subscribe to our Patreon!
(Scan the QR code or click if eBook)

**Visit our Linktree for
all social media sites!**
(Scan the QR code or click if eBook)

Download our catalog!
(Scan the QR code or click if eBook)

ABOUT THE AUTHORS

NIKKI NOIR is an author, editor, and publisher. She writes extreme horror, erotic thrillers, dark romance, and anything distinctly dark. Her fiction can be found on Godless, Blood Bound Books, and Amazon. Living in the Arizona desert, she finds any excuse to remain indoors hence why she became a writer with a full time job in IT & Security, hiding behind a computer all hours of the day. Besides working on a dozen projects at any given time, she is an avid reader, reviewer, dog cuddler (miniature dachshunds), baker/cake decorator, artist, gamer (console), and coffee connoisseur. Nikki can be found on Facebook, Instagram, TikTok, and Twitter @nikkinoirauthor. Find out more about Nikki at thatspookybeach.com.

STEVEN PAJAK, a Chicago-based author, crafts stories that explore the depths of horror and the human psyche. With a pen that dances on the edges of darkness, Steven brings to life tales that challenge, terrify, and linger in the minds of readers. Drawing inspiration from the urban tapestry of Chicago, his work merges the pulse of city life with the eerie quiet of the shadows lurking within the darkest corners of our minds. Steven invites you into a world where fear meets courage, and the journey through his imagination proves as haunting as it is unforgettable. Find out more about Steven at stevenpajak.com.

MEGAN STOCKTON is an indie author who lives in Grimsley, Tennessee, with her two children and her husband, who is an indie filmmaker. She writes in a variety of genres that all have dark/horror elements, and all of her work is character-driven and immersive. She is known for delivering works that are raw, thought-provoking, brutal, and cinematic. She has been writing since she was a child and was always obsessed with horror and the macabre. When she isn't writing (or working her day job), she likes to work with the animals on their farm, read, play video games, and watch movies. Find out more about Megan at www.meganstocktonbooks.com.

R.E. SARGENT is an editor, publisher, and author whose works delve into the sinister depths of horror, suspense, and the supernatural. His story "Lucy," featured in the Splatterpunk Award–nominated anthology *If I Die Before I Wake Volume 3 – Tales of Deadly Women and Retribution*, also resides among the dark tales in his collection, *Everything Went to Shit*. Nestled in the hauntingly beautiful Pacific Northwest, R.E. lives with his wife, their two granddogs, and the unyielding rain—a perfect companion for someone who revels in the eerie. Beneath the perpetual gray skies, he crafts stories that reach beyond the ordinary into realms best left undisturbed. Find out more about R.E. at resargent.com.

9 781964 398808